My Heart Still Beats for You

My Heart Still Beats for You

Tina Marie

www.urbanbooks.net

Urban Books, LLC
300 Farmingdale Road, N.Y.-Route 109
Farmingdale, NY 11735

My Heart Still Beats for You
Copyright © 2023 Tina Marie

ISBN 13: 978-1-64556-476-8
ISBN 10: 1-64556-476-2

First Trade Paperback Printing May 2023
Printed in the United States of America

10 9 8 7 6 5 4 3 2 1

*This is a work of fiction. Any references or similarities
to actual events, real people, living or dead, or to real
locales are intended to give the novel a sense of reality.
Any similarity in other names, characters, places, and
incidents is entirely coincidental.*

Distributed by Kensington Publishing Corp.
Submit Orders to:
Customer Service
400 Hahn Road
Westminster, MD 21157-4627
Phone: 1-800-733-3000
Fax: 1-800-659-2436

My Heart Still Beats for You

by

Tina Marie

Acknowledgments

I would first like to thank God for giving me this gift of writing and for providing me with every blessing I have received thus far and will receive in the future.

I want to thank my family for putting up with all the late nights and my crazy moods while I am writing. To my kids: Jashanti and Jasheer, I want you to know that I work so hard so you can have it all.

To my Cole Hart Presents team, salute to all of you for keeping on the grind and staying positive. Cole, the fact that you wanted me on your team means more to me than you will ever know. Princess and Anna, I swear you ladies are just amazing and I love you! Twyla, there is no category for someone like you. Anytime I need a shoulder, a friend, or a talking-to you are there. I know you are sick of me but I'ma love you foreverrrrrr! Jammie and Reese, you two truly just make my life complete, and I thank God for giving me friends like you. I want to thank all my Pen Sisters, no matter what company you are in, for all of the love, support, and for always helping to push me to my next goal. I appreciate you all!

To my mentor, T Styles, and the woman who can do it all, Charisse, I am amazed by you both, and my love for you two is unending.

Chan, I can never find a way to thank you for all the phone calls, late-night sessions, and just the unending support. It is more than appreciated. Just know you will always have a place in my heart. XOXO!

Acknowledgments

Shout out to the Prolific Pens, my family in Pen. We are taking this industry by storm. I hope the world is ready.

To my test readers, there would be no book without you ladies, you all are my blessings! Liz I couldn't ask for a better promoter~ one thing I learned in this business is it takes a team and finding you completed my team. To my Hitta's I could not and would not want to drop these books without y'all in my corner. I am sending you soo much love!

To my Clubhouse family I really would not have made it this year without y'all. You have a special place in my heart and have done more for me than you can ever imagine. XOXO!

To my Britt Brat aka Brittnee Chanel . . . this book would not have happened without you. From the cover to the title, you had my back as you always do! I love you boo!

To my friends and family: I appreciate all of the love and support. My cousins, Claire & Tanisha. My friends: Letitia, Natasha, Reese, Law, Sharome, Shante, Diana, and Kia. I'm truly grateful for you all, and I love you. To my best friend, there will never be enough letters in the alphabet to thank you for everything, so I won't even try.

To all my fans, readers, test readers, admins and anyone who has ever read or purchased my work, shared a link or a book cover, you're all appreciated, and I promise to keep pushing on your behalf to write what you're looking for.

Chapter 1

Phantom

"Son, I guess this little get-together is a wrap," I said, hugging my auntie and giving Dana a look, letting her know she was not off the fucking hook. I wasn't about to sit around and let anyone diss my girl, so when shawty said it was time to go, we were out. That fucking Dana's mouth was reckless, and Sahnai got what she deserved. I loved it when a ho tried to call another female a ho. I didn't care that Lox loved her. She chose a man over her kids and another man who loved her. She was selfish, and now she wanted to come for my woman, talking behind her back about our baby? *Get the fuck out of here.* I wasn't standing for that shit, and as everyone knew, I busted females' asses just like I would a nigga's, so she was just lucky my bae got her ass first.

Making sure Azia and the boys left out the front door before me, I told Azia to go home and start packing some clothes for her and the boys and to bring bathing suits. That stopped her from cursing and threatening Sahnai for a few minutes.

"Phantom, where we going and for how long? Is there a mall nearby? I think me and Inaya need a shopping day. She gonna need some bigger clothes and all, because I know your baby gonna have a big-ass head." She laughed.

I decided to take my little family out of town. We needed to get away from this drama and have some fun.

"Find an indoor waterpark or some shit. Somewhere we can drive to so we can leave ASAP, and use my Amex to book it. I want to be leaving tonight."

Before I could finish, she had the boys in the car and her face in her phone looking for places. Yeah, any chance Azia got to swipe one of my cards made her happy. I knew she also wanted to spend time with Iny. Those two were thick as thieves.

Only things I felt bad about were the kids having to see Sahnai get fucked up and that Iny's feelings had to get hurt. Yeah, I didn't give a fuck about what people thought, but I could see it in Inaya's eyes. She wasn't expecting that low blow from her own people. She'd been through a lot but was just now learning one of life's most important lessons—family will turn on you first.

Not wanting to upset her in front of Kadia, I put Kades in the truck and turned on the DVD player I had installed just for her. Closing the door, I grabbed Iny before she could get in, and I pulled her close. At first I could feel her pulling away, since she still claimed she didn't want a nigga, but I just tugged a little harder, and she fell into my arms.

"Ma, it's okay. Fuck Sahnai. You got me, Kades, and our baby. And don't forget Azia and the boys and, shit, even Lox. He loves your little ass. That nigga always talking 'bout why Sahnai can't be like you and you perfect and a good girl. I be having to threaten him all the time to stay out your face and kill any dreams he got because you belong to me. You don't need Sahnai for shit. We are your family."

Looking up at me with her big brown eyes, she began to cry.

"Phantom, do you believe what Dana said? Do you think this is not your baby or that I went with Noah willingly?"

Fuck. How do I tell her I believe her without telling her about the pictures and the videos?

"Ma, look, I know that's my fucking baby. I knew you was gone before you even took the test. Sleeping all day and shit, eating pineapples in your salad with ranch. Look, I don't let shit people say affect me, and I seen the place Noah had you at, and, ma, I'ma be honest. He sent me pictures . . ." I had to pause because I could feel a tear drop onto her cheek. Mingling with her tear, sharing her pain, I stopped a minute just watching it.

"Iny, he sent me pics of you tied up and him beating you and more, just to fuck wit' me. I am so sorry you had to go through that. I am sorry I didn't protect you and Kadia. I fucked up and will never forgive myself, and I promise I am never leaving your side. I got your back through it all." Not even letting her respond to what I felt was bullshit, I rubbed her little belly, and then I pulled her a little closer so she could feel my heart beat and my man grinding into her pussy. He was only separated by her little-ass yellow summer dress and a nude silk thong that, if she would let me, could just be slid to the side. Taking a chance, I leaned down and kissed the side of her face, then made my way to her lips. As soon as my tongue touched hers, her whole body loosened up, and I knew then that her mind was no longer on Sahnai or her rape or Dana. It was fully on me. Suddenly we were interrupted by a tiny voice.

"Mommy, Daddy, are we leaving yet? I am hungry."

Laughing, we both stepped away and went to get in the truck.

"That is what I want to hear, ma—laughter. Now let's get all my babies something to eat and then go home and pack. I am taking us on a vacation. We need to get the hell out of here."

"Jahdair, where are we going? I am happy. I need to get away from all of this, plus Kadia deserves a vacation after all that she has been through. Oh, yeah, and, Phantom, book us separate rooms please. Remember we are not together."

Cutting my eyes at her, I responded, "Ma, we together. You just not on board yet, so dead that separate rooms shit. As a matter of fact, I am going to have Kadia stay in the room with Azia and the boys. I don't know where we going yet. Call Azia and find out so you know what to pack." Glancing back at Kadia to make sure she had on her headphones, I decided to throw one last comment out there. "Iny, you know you miss daddy all up in that stuff, so stop pouting," I teased her, laughing.

Mushing me with one hand and dialing Azia with the other, all I heard was her telling my sister I was an asshole, and my sister just laughed and agreed.

"Azia, where are we going, sis?"

"Splash Lagoon. It's this indoor water spot in Pennsylvania. So pack a bathing suit. You better wear it while you can because once that baby takes over your body, it's over for you, especially if it's a boy. Oooh, wait, there is an outlet nearby, so pack light."

Snatching the phone even though it was on speaker, I had already heard enough. "Azia, order pizza so we have food when we get there. Kadia is hungry, and I am sure the boys are too. Azia, listen good. Pack all you need. No more damn shopping."

Hanging up the phone this time, Inaya was the one giggling. She was hunched over in the seat, facing the window and hoping I wouldn't see.

"Yo, don't be all scrunched up hurting my son and shit, and I know you ain't laughing at me. I meant it. No fucking shopping." Even though I said it, if shopping would bring a smile to Iny's face, fuck it. She could spend all my shit.

Once we pulled into the complex, I started thinking about buying a house for Inaya and the kids. We were living in the suburbs, but my kids needed more space, and since Azia wanted to sell her house and move here to be near her sister, as she called Inaya (I guessed it was "fuck her big brother"), maybe I could find some houses close together. I was going to talk to Inaya after this little trip.

I felt one of my phones vibrate and thought it was Lox. I looked down to tell that nigga to hurry and get ready because Azia found a spot for us to get away. I decided that he and his new lady, Alani, should come with us on the little family vacay. Knowing I had to make a few moves before we left, I carried a sleeping Kadia in the house and set her on the couch.

"Yo, Inaya, we gonna be gone for a week, so pack what y'all need, and if you forget some shit, don't worry. You can go shopping."

"Oh, she can go shopping, huh? But you talk shit to me. This is so fucking unfair," mumbled Azia, interrupting me. Laughing at how she poked her lips out, I turned back to Iny to focus on her.

"Anyway, before we got interrupted by princess over there, I gotta make some runs, but I will be back in a few hours." Leaning close to her, I touched her belly and leaned closer to kiss her cheek. I whispered, "I love you," before I turned to walk away. I thought I said it so she didn't hear it, but the look on her face didn't let me know shit.

Trying to push Inaya out of my mind so I could focus on business was not easy. Sliding into my BMW, I sank down in the leather seat and ran my hand over my face. I was so happy to be getting away. This nigga Tae was going to have to hold it down while I was gone. He was a young cat, but he was thorough and loyal, and that was what mattered. After that bullshit with Lamar, I was doing an audit of these niggas on my team, and anyone else who wanted to be Billy Badass was going to end up floating next to Lamar's bitch ass.

Chapter 2

Inaya

Getting my suitcase out next door, I began putting in all of my bathing suits and a bunch of sundresses, shorts, and baby-doll tees. I threw in sandals, flip-flops, and a few sweatsuits in case the weather was cold at night. Kadia was easy to pack for, so before an hour had passed, I was done. Looking in the mirror, I could see all the stress was getting to me from the past few months. I didn't even feel like I was pretty anymore. I knew Phantom must feel sorry for me to have said he wanted me looking how I looked. We were not leaving until seven, so I decided to go to the hair shop real quick and do something with this mess. I texted my hairdresser, Mya, and she said she would squeeze me in and to just come through.

Pulling up to the hair shop on Dewey, I jumped out of Phantom's Audi, still my favorite car to drive even though he bought me a truck. I sat in the chair, waiting to be washed or something.

"Mya, I want something totally different. I want a brand-new look."

"Okay, I got you, but it's gonna be a big change, so don't freak out when you see it. Sit back and relax, and no looking in any fucking mirrors until I am done."

Feeling all kinds of stuff being rubbed into my hair, then having it washed out, I was curious about what was happening. Scrolling through Facebook on my phone, I stopped short when I saw chunks of hair hit the floor next to my chair. *Damn, I never thought she would cut it.* Sitting under the dryer, I felt my hairdresser next to me and realized she had her waxing stuff out so I could get these bushy eyebrows done. *Thank God.* I was starting to look like a monkey. Another hour later I was finished. She spun my chair around. I couldn't believe how much better I looked. Shoot, I didn't even recognize myself I looked so good. My hair was cut short into an edgy look. Some of the hair was somewhat covering my eyes and forehead in a slight swoop. I had never had short hair, and I loved it. My cheekbones stood out, and with my freshly waxed eyebrows, I looked like a model.

"Mya, I love it! I don't even recognize myself. I never would have thought to cut my hair, shoot, especially not this short, but it looks so good on me. How much do I owe you?"

"Aww, I am glad you love it. I was scared to keep cutting after I started and seen the look on your face. You was over there looking like a deer in headlights who was ready to run. It will be seventy-five dollars, hon."

Handing her a $100 bill, I hugged her and walked next door to the nail shop. I kept my toes done, but I rarely painted my nails, but since my hair was looking so nice, I decided to say fuck it and do both. An hour later, with pink toes, one with fake diamonds on it, and matching pink gel nails on my fingers, I drove home happy and singing for no reason. I knew the reason though: Phantom. He always made me happy even when he made me sad. Feeling my phone vibrate I figured it

was Phantom calling, so I just hit answer on the car's Bluetooth without looking.

"Hello. I am on my way back if you need me to pick up anything. I packed for you too if you don't mind," I said.

"Hello? Inaya, where you going, and what nigga you packing for if it ain't me?"

Hearing Cudjie's voice I almost hit a fire hydrant.

"Hey, Cudjie, sorry. I thought you were someone else. Anyway, what's up? How you been?"

"Well? Fuck you thought I was, baby girl? That fuck-ass brother of mine, Phantom? Ha. I heard how happy your ass sounded when you thought it was that nigga. When you realized it was me, you sounded like your dog died and shit," he taunted me, laughing.

Wait, brother? Since when are he and Phantom brothers? If he is Phantom's brother, that means he is Azia's brother too, I guess. Unless Phantom's mom has an outside son. Now that I think about it, I can see a slight resemblance to Phantom when I look at Cudjie, except Cudjie's ass is ugly, and he has those small rat ears.

"So what if I did think it was Phantom? Why you mad? You jealous or something, nigga?"

"Nah. What I'm mad for? If I wanted to just fuck you like he did, I would have done it already. I am trying to build something wit' you, ma, but you don't listen. You hardheaded. First, this nigga caused your daughter to be taken, and then tortured, but you still fucking wit' him. Now you home waiting by the phone for a nigga who is wit' another bitch right now, riding around wit' her and all. All this time and he has a girl, and guess what, Inaya. It's not you!"

Pulling up to the house, I could see that Phantom still hadn't made it back. I called him while I was still in the parking lot so no one else could see my emotions or be in his and my business. Hearing the phone ring, like, three times, I was about to hang up. *I guess he is with a bitch because he isn't answering my call, and normally he answers on the first ring.* As I was hanging up, I heard his sexy voice.

"Hey, babe, you and my kids good?"

Feeling happy again, I replied, "Hey, I just went and got my hair done. I hope you don't mind I used the money you had in the bedside table, and I painted my toes. We are all packed and ready. Just waiting on you and Lox."

"Iny, my money is your money. You supposed to be getting your hair and nails done and shit. I got a surprise for you, too."

I heard a female voice in the background. "Phantom, baby, get off the phone. This our time."

I was crushed. It felt like someone punched me in the chest, and I couldn't breathe.

"Iny, I'ma be home in a minute as soon as I am done handling this business." Phantom rushed me off the phone with his lame-ass excuse and hung up.

I guess Cudjie is right. I mean, shit, he would know. That is his brother. I can't say shit anyway. I am not his woman or his girlfriend. I am just his baby mama.

Walking in the house, the first thing I noticed was that Lox was already there, and the next was Kadia and another little girl jumping around, yelling, "Let's go, let's go," at the top of their lungs.

"Oh, my God, Iny, what did you do to your hair? I love it," squealed Azia as she ran over to touch it.

"Azia, don't touch," I yelled at her, joking around.

"Wow, Inaya, Phantom is going to love the new look on you. Let me introduce you to my girl. Alani, this is Phantom's girl, Inaya. Inaya, this is Alani and her daughter, Vivy."

Alani was cute, like "Cover Girl, I don't need no makeup" cute. She was a light brown color with naturally curly hair pulled into two intricate-looking braids. She was a little shorter than me and had on a cute white romper with cute white sandals. Yeah, she was good for Lox. I could see he really liked her by the way he kept looking at her face and not her ass.

"It's nice to finally meet you, Inaya. I hear about you all the time, and I love Kadia. She comes to play with Vivy at the house with the other kids. I hope you don't take this the wrong way, but how the fuck you tolerate mean-ass Phantom long enough to have kids with him?"

Saying that, she smiled, and I didn't even feel no way about it. It was kind of funny because that nigga was mean.

Laughing, I replied, "Girl, I don't know. Phantom can be a handful, but he is a great dad, and he is sweet when he wants to be. I mean, I am nervous for the doctors and nurses when I give birth to this one and he is in the room because his mouth is reckless. I guess at least I will have something to laugh about."

"What nigga mouth is reckless, Inaya? You talking to another nigga and you carrying my baby? A'ight, I'ma fuck you and him up." Phantom came in talking shit, but the way he was smiling, he knew we were all talking about his ass. "All right, everybody, let's go. We are all going to Splash Lagoon to have a nice little family getaway."

The kids ran for the door, and even li'l Q was laughing and dragging his little Polo duffle bag.

I told Phantom I wanted to ride with the girls going down, and he and Lox should each drive one of their cars to fit all the kids and me, and the girls should drive alone so we could have a break. Lox's mom stayed home with Aiden. He had been sick a lot lately, so they thought it was best for him not to come. Phantom was nice enough to go and pick up my little cousin Nadia so she could come with us too. I really only wanted to ride with the girls so I could talk to Azia about Cudjie and this whole situation. I asked to get in the back of the car so I could curl my pregnant ass up with this fluffy pink and orange blanket I brought. *This baby is making me sleepy all the time. I just can't hang anymore.*

While I was getting ready to climb in the back of Azia's Benz truck, Phantom came and stopped me.

"Damn, ma, come give your nigga a hug or something since you don't want to ride wit' me. I thought you was my ride or die," he said while pulling me close to him. I could smell his Armani cologne, and it was making my panties wet. He hadn't tried to have sex with me since I had been back. I didn't know if he was just not interested anymore or he was trying to give me time. Thinking about him and that girl today made me lean more toward the possibility that he was just not interested.

Laying my head on his chest, I could feel his heartbeat. Even though everyone was waiting on us and watching us, it felt like it was only him and me. It felt like time stopped. I could feel his breath next to my ear and his soft lips on my cheek then my neck.

"Yo, that new hairstyle you got, I love it. You look sexy as fuck. I mean, you was already sexy, but now I can see your pretty face, and it's got that pregnancy glow. I just wanna rip off these tights you got on and go all in. We gotta get on the road before it gets too late. Inaya, think about me, ma, and take care of my baby." Lightly kissing my lips, he helped me in the back and went to start driving.

"Okay, Inaya, what is going on? I know you wasn't really trying to ride with us and leave your boo, so tell me, what's up?"

"Damn, sis, you know me now?" I asked while laughing. *Shit, she know she got me, living all in my fucking mind at times.* She just looked at me in the rearview mirror as if to say she was waiting. "Look, Alani, I am sorry. We just met, but I don't really have anyone right now but Azia, and I have to get this off my chest because I have been going through a lot."

"Girl, we are like family now. I heard about you and your daughter being kidnapped, and I could not imagine going through that. You are strong. You never hesitated to go and save her all by yourself, so if you need somebody, that's fine. I don't mind being one of those people."

Crying, I began with the call I got from Cudjie before I went to find Kadia. "Cudjie called me out of the blue and was asking me if I was okay. When I told him what happened with Kadia, he asked me how Noah and Phantom knew each other, and I explained I didn't know. This is the thing that is confusing me. Cudjie said that Noah and Phantom were friends. Then today Cudjie told me Phantom was with another woman and that he would know because Phantom was his brother. I thought Cudjie was his worker, not his brother."

"How do you know Cudjie? He is our brother, but he is not someone you should be around. He doesn't care about anyone but himself, and he is actually pretty dangerous. He let one of his baby moms take a drug charge for him while she was pregnant. She didn't even know he had drugs coming to her house. His three-year-old son he once left at a Chuck E. Cheese alone all day and came back to pick him up after he hung out with another woman to find someone had called the police and child protective services. He also hates Phantom more than anything, mainly because he wants to be him, so he will tell you anything," Azia finished telling me with a shake of her head.

"But, Azia, this is the fucked-up thing. After he told me Phantom was with another woman, I called Phantom, and a bitch was in the back asking him to get off the phone because he was allowing the call to interrupt their time together."

"What did he say after that?" asked Alani.

"He told me he was handling business and would be home in a few, then hung up in my face."

"Hell no! I know he is my brother, but he is out of line. I don't know why these men cannot leave trashy women alone once they find a good one. He must like being alone. Inaya, don't let him hurt you or treat you like shit. Fuck it, leave him alone. We can both go look for a new man once you drop that baby."

"I know I don't know you that well, but I can tell you love Phantom, so I know it won't be that easy to just brush him off or move on to the next. So what are you going to do?"

"Alani, I honestly don't know. Now some female is calling and telling me to stay away from her man and hanging up. I just thought things would finally get settled in my life. I pushed my internship off until September due to all that has happened, and I was just starting to let Phantom back into my heart, but now . . . I just don't know."

The rest of the ride was filled with us chatting about everything while we got to know Alani. I really liked her.

She was funny and insightful. I must have fallen asleep, because before I knew it, I was being woken by Azia.

"Princess Sleepyhead, we there, so wake your ass up."

Walking in, I was excited for the kids. They were sleepy since it was late but still smiling and talking about all the stuff they were going to do tomorrow. I was kind of dreading being alone with Phantom. I was hoping he would keep Kadia in with us, but before I could hold on to that dream, Azia grabbed all the kids in a line, turned, winked at me and Alani, and made her way to their suite.

Chapter 3

Lox

Watching the kids play in the water, I couldn't remember a time I was this happy. Shit, maybe when I was small and we were back in Jamaica. I was always happy then. I felt like I was free, and now I felt like I was free again. Free of all these random women and unhappy, sneaking-ass baby mamas. Alani didn't want to give a nigga a chance at all, but I broke her down. I still remembered the look on her face when I just showed up at her front door and took her and Vivy with me for the day. She had so much fun at the house, and my mom loved her. We swam all day and all went to Golden Corral to eat.

Watching her chasing Q and Vivy through the water spray in her little-ass sky blue bikini with clear rhinestones on it, I had to look away because I didn't want to have my dick showing through these swim shorts in front of all the little kids and shit. I couldn't wait until later to take her in the Jacuzzi in the room and dig in those guts again. We didn't sleep a bit at all last night. I hoped whoever was in the room next door didn't hear us, because I had her little ass screaming for help and to not stop at the same time.

Seeing the phone vibrate next to me, I snatched it up when I saw Toya's name flash across the screen.

"Yo, I been fucking calling you like crazy for a week. You not worried something is wrong with our fucking son?"

"Lox, why you gotta be yelling at me and shit? I am the mother of your child, and I don't deserve to be talked to like this. I have been busy working and taking care of my other children. If you don't remember, I am pregnant, and this pregnancy has been very rough on me. Shit, this is your cousin's baby, so you should not be stressing me out when I am carrying his baby."

"Bitch, you're stupid. Phantom said it ain't his kid, and since him and his girl have a baby on the way, I need you to back off. I called you because our son is underweight for his age and always sick. I mean, very sick. Is there something wrong with him that you failed to tell me? I am still waiting on your lazy ass to send me his medical records." I yelled the last part because it was only two and a half minutes into the conversation and she was getting on my fucking nerves.

"Well, I do remember the doctors wanted to run tests because they thought he may have some sickness, an autoimmune disease or something that is causing his immune system to fail. He stopped getting sick, so I never bothered with the tests." As she poured out the last excuse, I hung up in her face. Getting up, I needed to go and get some air. Just like that, all the happiness of a few minutes ago was gone and replaced with stress.

I couldn't believe my baby might have a serious illness. I didn't want any one of my kids to suffer or be in pain. Calling his pediatrician to set up appointments for testing and give him the information, I just sat outside on the bench with my head in my hands.

I felt her soft hands on my back and her skin next to my face. She didn't even speak. She just came up next to me and held me.

"Babe, Toya just called me and told me the doctors thought Aiden may have some autoimmune disease, and she never got him tested because she thought it went away. I am so disgusted with her. How much more irresponsible can a person be? Why is it women like her are even blessed with children and then they treat them like shit?"

"Lennox, look, I know this is frustrating and scary, but I promise we will get through this. I got your back, and all it takes is a team, and we are a team." With that, she kissed me on the head and went back in. *Damn, I am lucky to find one like her. I know that means I have to stop giving in to Sahnai and fucking her when I see her. I have to totally let go of her because the love we once shared was the love of young people, and I have outgrown it.*

Heading back in, I played with the kids in the water for a while, and then Alani, Azia, Phantom, and I played water volleyball. Inaya sat on the side of the pool being the referee and pouting every few minutes because Phantom would not let her play. Watching the two of them, I was happy Iny gave Phantom a lot of chances. I knew he loved her the first day he spoke to her and stalked Kadia's bus so he could take them for ice cream. I never saw my cousin go out of his way for any woman who was not my mom or his sister. I just hoped he didn't fuck it up. He still kicked it with that little bitch Ashena sometimes and probably a few others too.

"Inaya, why you mad? Your boo got you on lockdown?" I teased her, causing her to hit me in the back of the head with the ball. Good thing I had all that fucking hair. I splashed her and she splashed me back, causing Alani to splash her, and before I knew it, we were having a mini water fight. Seeing that Iny was getting tired, Phantom picked up on it quick and grabbed her right up and took her to their room, leaving the rest of us to go grab the kids and take them to get ready for bed. Tomorrow, we were taking them to the arcade downstairs and laser tag.

"Lox, you think that Phantom is good for Inaya?"

"Azia, come on now, of course he is. He has never been this way before. He is so happy when he is with her and Kadia and shit, he is like a whole new person now. The old him would have never been into no shit like this or he would have already offended all the staff here that he didn't fuck and then offend later," I replied.

"See, Lox, that's what I mean. She is good for him, but is he good for her?" Azia threw at me and then walked away with the kids. *Damn, I hope cuz is not fucking up with Inaya. I bet that is why she wanted to ride with the girls. Something is up, and I'm going to ask Alani after I tear that ass up again tonight.*

"Alani, come in the shower wit' me, girl. Let me wash you up."

"You ain't slick, nigga. You want to get dirty, not wash up. But I'ma come anyway because I love getting dirty wit' you." With that, her bikini was on the floor, and she beat me to the shower. Pushing her against the wall, I began licking on her perfect little breasts. They were not too big but just right for my mouth. Then I moved my fingers to her pussy and felt her dripping wet.

"Lani, I love that you are always ready for me." Pushing my way in, I couldn't help but moan a little. Her shit was so tight. Turning her over, I spread her ass cheeks wide and let the tip of my dick just rub against her clit.

"Lox, give it to me, baby. Stop playing and put it in. Shitttt, I am about to cum."

Hearing that was all I needed. I dove in as deep as I could and let my dick do all the talking. Pulling her hair, I knew I couldn't hold out much longer. Pulling out to nut on her back, I fell against the wall of the shower, bringing her with me.

"Fuck, you got some good-ass pussy, girl. I can't go without this shit." She was so worn out she didn't even talk any shit, just smiled and kissed my chest. Washing us up so we could get out and get in the bed, I thanked God for giving me Alani.

Chapter 4

Phantom

Sitting in my Range looking at the house with Cudjie walking in and out, I was trying to decide if I was going to kill my brother today. He was trying to fuck up my money, which was bad enough, but the shit he told Inaya . . . *I mean, fuck!* He tried to take away the best fucking thing I had ever had. From day one, Inaya loved me and trusted me even when I talked to her slick as fuck and put her down. When she came home, I knew something was up because she kept pulling away, but I didn't imagine it was no shit like this.

I was thankful as hell that Azia told me everything Inaya had been telling her. She had been telling me to leave Iny alone for a while, but I guessed now that we had a baby on the way, she had a change of heart, because she was doing everything to keep us together. Knowing that Inaya had been carrying around all this hurt that I caused her by me still sleeping with Ashena for so long and she never even said a word cut me deep inside. It was like, instead of being loud and ratchet and coming to attack me or cuss me out, she just started to fade away. Fade out of my life. I still saw her every day, but when we spoke, it wasn't the same. She answered my question with no real emotion. *I can't take this shit.* Now that I knew what was up, I could see the hurt in her eyes when she looked at me. One day when I was leaving to give Ashena a ride from work, I thought she was going to say something about it, but she changed her mind and sadly walked away.

Ashena is next after I deal with Cudjie's bitch ass. She couldn't just keep her dick suckers closed. No, she had to become the side chick from every urban book and movie. The one who couldn't stay in her place and started fucking with the main one. Calling Inaya's phone and hanging up, sending her pictures, and shit. I didn't even treat Ashena with one ounce of like, respect, or anything. I didn't take her ass out. I didn't tell her she was pretty, or I loved her, fuck, or even liked her. I saw her, fucked her, or let her suck my man, and that was it. Yet she was still telling people she and I were together and that I was her man. *Get the fuck out of here.* These bitches were psycho.

Seeing a number come up on my phone that said Strong Hospital, I answered right away thinking something was wrong with Inaya or Kadia. "Yo."

"Phantom, I need you to get up here. I am about to give you your first real child, and I don't want you to miss it."

"Toya? Girl, I already fucking told you I ain't your baby daddy. I'ma stop through there tomorrow to get that DNA work done. No need to worry about that. On the strength of you bringing my daughter back to me, I want to wish you all the best." Hanging up, I decided to save Cudjie for another day and go home to check on Inaya. It was time she and I had a real talk about all of this. I didn't like her feeling hurt. *Maybe I should let her go.* She needed a nine-to-five nigga, one who would not cheat on her or get mad and call her stupid or some other shit. I couldn't be that perfect nigga. I was scared of this shit called love, so I kept sleeping with other chicks. Settling down was not for me, so here I went to break up with Inaya, again.

Walking into Inaya's place where she started staying when we came back from Splash Lagoon, all the lights were off, and the house was pretty quiet except for the low sound of the TV in the living room. Kadia was at summer camp right now, so I guessed that was why it was so quiet. Smiling when I walked in the living room, I saw Iny sleeping on the couch with some little-ass Nike Pro Shorts on that were so tight on her I could see her pussy print. She had her hands tucked under her head and had fallen asleep watching one of her favorite movies, *Dirty Dancing*. Inaya was a romantic and always had me watching some movie with people falling in love.

I picked her up to put her upstairs in the bed, and she woke up and looked startled.

"Is Kadia okay?" she asked quickly with fear in her eyes. I hated that because of me she had that fear in her eyes.

"She is good, ma. I wanted to see you. I missed you and our baby. Seems like you have been avoiding me lately. You won't even let me stay the night anymore. What's up?"

"Nothing, Phantom. I am good and the baby is good. I am sick all the time, so I don't want to bother you or interrupt your sleep. It's better for me to stay over here without you," she said, moving out of my arms and going to the couch farther away to sit back down. Following her, I got on the floor right in front of her and put my arms on both sides of her so I was blocking her in.

"Look, Inaya, I know you found out I be fucking around this bitch named Ashena sometimes. I don't know what to say. I mean, I am sorry. I really don't know how you feel about the situation, ma, since you not really saying much lately, just pushing me away."

Seeing her face scrunch up, I thought she was going to cry, but instead she pulled herself together and began to speak.

"Jahdair, how do you expect me to feel? I fucking love you. I feel like shit. I feel hurt that the man I love won't even fuck me anymore but is all over this other bitch. I cry myself to sleep because she is sending me pictures of the two of you fucking or her sucking your dick, and yeah, I know it's you because of the scar you have on your belly and the tattoo of the crown you have. I am not stupid. I know I am not a big ol' freak in the bed, and I guess I am not that pretty. I don't know what this girl has to offer you, but obviously you can't stay away from it. I feel like I can't breathe most days, and I cry and cry, and I don't know how to stop. I feel stupid for loving someone who doesn't love me back. That's how the fuck I feel."

Watching her run upstairs, I followed but stopped outside of her bedroom door. Standing there listening to her cry, I realized I couldn't keep hurting her like this. I loved her more than myself, and I was never going to change, so I had to walk out of her life for good.

Running down the stairs and next door to my crib, I went in my room to pack some shit. *I'ma go check on business I have in Arizona and Florida for a while. This will give Inaya some time to forget about me. I'm out as soon as I pay Toya's trick ass a visit to see if this is my kid, and then I'ma deal with Ashena. Man, she was sending Iny pictures. Fuck. This shit is out of control. I should have never started messing with her again.*

"Phantom, where the hell you think you going? What did you do?" Azia stood in my doorway with her hands on her hips, staring at me like a mother would.

"Yo, go next door and check on Inaya. I hurt her again, and I am leaving. I can't keep breaking her heart. I haven't said it, but I love her, and I don't like to hurt the ones I love. She is everything to me, but I keep fucking up, and she is better off with someone else."

Pushing past Azia, I ran right out the front door to her calling my name. Looking at Inaya's window one last time, I threw the keys to the Audi in her mailbox and texted Azia to give her those since she loved the car so much, and then I hurried to my truck before I changed my mind. That was not an option right now. I couldn't allow Inaya to break my heart if I told her how I felt, so leaving was the best I could do for both of us.

Chapter 5

Sahnai

I had fucked up so much since I had been back in Rochester, back around Lox. I knew my actions caused him to hurt, and now that I was done with Honest, I wanted him and my family back. Yeah, I knew he had somebody, and I had to admit she seemed like a good one, but fuck that. I didn't care. Lox was mine first, and I didn't give a fuck about him so-called trying to move on or none of that shit. I also was not with him allowing that bitch to play mommy to my son. I knew it was shady, but if he didn't get rid of her, I would.

Picking up my iPhone 6 and maneuvering my nails around the sparkly gems decorating my case, I went to my favorites and clicked on the picture of Lox and me at a park with Q. While the phone was ringing, I began putting my clothes in my brown Louis suitcase. *If Lox doesn't fall into line with what I want, his new girl will be seeing a video of him and me making the sweetest love.* Yeah, I did that. The last time he came over and fucked me, I intentionally made sure I was recording that shit and saved the video for later use. See, Lennox got me fucked up thinking he could fuck me and then toss me to the side after all we'd been through.

Yeah, my feelings were hurt that he made that light-skinned bitch his girl, and they hadn't even been through shit. Back when it was him and me in the Bronx, we made shit happen. I used to watch his back in the streets no matter what. Even when he and I were beefing. I remembered one morning he woke me up by snatching me out of the bed, screaming and yelling, asking me who the fuck was Mellow and why was he texting me at five a.m. While I was trying to explain that Mellow was a client of mine at the shop, I couldn't even get a word out because he was banging me around the room and tearing shit up. Due to all the noise, the upstairs neighbor called the police, and when they came, I made sure I was still naked in the room.

I told the officer I was okay. I just wanted to leave, but I needed to put some clothes on. As soon as they closed the door, I hid this nigga's gun in the floorboards under the bed and hid his money in my purse. After jumping into my clothes and quickly stashing in some shoes the little bags of cocaine he had lying around to sell, I was ready to go. Even though he busted my ass, I still protected him. *He has to love me more than this bitch. She doesn't even know him.*

"Hello. Hello, Sahnai, are you there?" Lox yelled into the phone. I forgot I was even on a call and daydreaming. His voice woke me up quick.

"Hey, baby, I am just calling you to see how you're doing."

"I'm cool, ma. What day you want the kids this week? I can drop them on Tuesday or Wednesday. The weekend is not gonna work though, because we are taking them to some Sesame Place shit."

"Babe, I called to talk to you about us. I miss you, and since the other day I can't stop thinking about us. Thinking about how it felt making love to you the other day. I know I fucked up accusing you of being with Toya again and not protecting me when I was stabbed. I realize now that Toya saved Kadia and had nothing to do with stabbing me at all. As a matter of fact, I think I know who stabbed me, and I am taking care of that situation."

Before I could continue, I heard Lox's deep voice laughing. At first, I thought maybe he was entertaining one of the kids, until he spoke again.

"Yo, Sahnai, you are tripping, ma. I don't know why you got the idea that there is ever going to be a you and me again. I mean, when I come by there, it is just to drop off the little ones and keep it movin'. I ain't had sex wit' you, and I don't plan on it ever again. I need you to not call me wit' no more bullshit like that again, especially when you know I got a good woman at home."

This nigga is really on some shit right now. I can't believe he wants to treat me like a jump off. I was already mad because I was over here struggling wit' one of my suitcases, and now this nonsense. I didn't ever remember feeling this frustrated. All this at once was too much for me. I felt like screaming at Lox, breaking down, and asking him why the fuck I was never good enough to be his girl. I held him down. I looked good, and I even gave him his first kid. He never even asked who was the one who stabbed me so he could go and handle that shit.

Instead of lowering myself to begging for answers or showing him that truly I was weak and broken inside without him and my kids, I just moved my freshly mani-cured pink nail over the end button and clicked. Going to messages and pulling up Alani's number, I sent her three videos I had saved on my phone and some text messages of Lox talking about missing me and my good, good pussy. Pushing the mint green sweater dress farther into my bag, I tugged on the gold zipper one final time, and it gave, but in the process, it cut my finger.

"Fuck!" I yelled out, hearing my voice echo in the empty room.

Seeing my phone buzz and Lox's name pop up, I clicked ignore, not even looking at the picture of him and Q like I usually did. Almost immediately, I saw the phone ring with a call from Honest, and he also got sent to voicemail. The text notifications began going off back-to-back. Phine sent me four, and I knew it was about his money I took. I didn't give a fuck. That was one of the reasons I was leaving for a while and doing it in a hurry. I was going to let shit die down. Pressing send on the message I was sending to Alani, I smiled thinking of how Lox even told me he loved me in the video. *Alani's heart will be broken, and she is going to leave him in the dust.*

Deciding to turn the annoying-ass phone off, I threw it down on the bed and made my way to the bathroom to wash the blood off of my finger. As soon as I was unwrapping one of little Q's dinosaur Band-Aids, the only kind I had in the medicine cabinet, to cover the cut I got from the zipper, I heard someone ringing my bell and banging on my door.

I immediately froze and hit the floor. My dumb ass left the curtains open, so anyone could see me standing in the doorway. Grabbing my two duffle bags—one with money and one with clothes—I began scooting across the floor to the stairs. Trying to creep down the stairs with two big-ass Louis Vuitton bags and a fucked-up finger was not easy, but I finally made it to the kitchen. *I bet it's Phine's bitch ass at the door. I guess he recovered from the special drink I gave him a lot faster than I thought he would. I'ma just wait until he leaves, and then I am out. I know Phine isn't going to stay out there knocking long, because he is a bitch, and as far as he knows, Honest is still a presence in my household.*

It had been quiet about twenty minutes, so I guessed he got the hint and left. As soon as my hand touched the front doorknob, the door flew open and knocked me on my ass. Looking up and expecting to see Phine, or even Lox, I was looking at Honest for some reason.

"Nigga, is you crazy busting my door off the fucking hinges and shit?" I said with an attitude as I walked into the kitchen to grab a bottle of water. Of all the dummies to pop up now, it would be this one. I knew he heard me the last time when I said I needed my space to get my kid back. Realizing he still hadn't said shit and that he was just standing there like a big-ass creep, I decided to let him know I was leaving.

"Honest, look, I know you care about me and stuff, but as I said before, we can't be doing this. I am focused on getting my son back and trying to mend fences with my family. Now as you can see, I am on my way out the door, the one you broke, by the way. So I will call you later." I breezed by him and headed to the front, bags in hand. Turning around, he appeared to be following, so that was a relief. Before I could even put my hand to the mangled knob, I felt a blow to the back of the head, and everything went dark.

Waking up what felt like hours later, I was in Honest's Range Rover, in the front seat. I tried to reach for my phone or hit this nigga one good time before I realized I couldn't move my hands. Looking down, I realized they were tied up with a thick white rope, and this brave moth-erfucker even put tape over my mouth. I wanted to laugh because this seemed like some Lifetime movie shit, and I wanted to cry for the same reason. *What the hell is going on?* It looked like we were heading toward Maryland, because I could see us passing all the landmarks I used to see on the backroads of Pennsylvania when I would drive back and forth—Texas Roadhouse and the Peebles department store. I even saw us fly by Reptile Land, so I knew the direction we were heading. I tried to read the expression on his face. He had a calm smile going and was humming to some R&B song on the radio. *Does he think we are going on a pleasant drive? I mean, he is kidnapping me. This is not a road trip.*

"We are almost there, so now I have to cover your eyes so the surprise isn't ruined."

Feeling a cloth come over my head, I suddenly couldn't see anything anymore. I felt like I couldn't breathe, and I began to struggle against the ropes. I tried pushing the tape off with my tongue, but all that did was leave a nasty chemical taste in my mouth from the sticky stuff. Feeling the car come to a stop, I finally felt relief. I could try to figure this out once I was not tied up and belted into a moving car. I was no punk, and eventually Honest was going to want to fuck, and I was going to have the upper hand. Some niggas couldn't understand no and "I don't want you anymore." Now I knew for sure he was the one who stabbed me in the park. Only someone as crazy as him would try that shit.

I could feel myself being carried into what I assumed was a house. I heard the front door slam and then a woman began talking.

"Damn, Christopher, it took you this long to bring her to me? Was you getting attached to her or what? Don't be falling in love with what belongs to me, Honest, do you fucking hear me?"

"Yo, shut the fuck up. Here she go, all nice and un-harmed. Yeah, the pussy was good, and I hope you letting me get it again, but there is no love. She had a bunch of people around her until she fucked up, so here she is."

After that was said, Christopher aka Honest threw me on the bed and began ripping my clothes off. I could feel my heart beating faster, like it was going to burst out of my chest. I felt his hands rubbing my legs, and then I felt another hand on my breast. This hand was soft and had long nails at the end. I could smell a fruity smell, like mangoes and strawberries, that had to be coming from her.

"Yes, Sahnai, I have waited a very long time for you," she said and laughed.

Chapter 6

Lox

I wished I could figure out what the fuck was wrong with this bitch Sahnai. I was not even the kind of dude to be calling females a bitch, but yeah, she was one. First, she ran away from me without a word, living off of niggas in the streets to take care of my seed, who I didn't even know about. Then she came back and abandoned me and our kid for some lame-ass nigga I didn't trust. I caught her on the phone saying she knew who stabbed her, but I wasn't into talking about that shit on the phone, because then, when a nigga came up missing, I didn't want my name in shit. Besides, she didn't have to say shit. I knew it was that nigga Honest from the moment he conveniently popped his fake, wannabe brown-skinned ass up at the hospital. I never understood these niggas out here using bleach on their skin like a fucking female or something. All those chemicals must have been getting to his brain if he thought he could fuck with my baby moms and not get what was coming to him.

Now she was on my line, threatening my relationship with Alani. Running my hands through my dreads, I took a deep breath before standing up to get out of the bed. I could hear the boys downstairs giggling and Alani singing "The Wheels on the Bus." That was why I loved her. She was a go-with-the-flow kind of girl, and she loved my sons even though the circumstances with them were not the best. Two different moms, and both of them could have been better to the boys, but Alani just stepped in and stepped up. She never mentioned Toya or Sahnai except to ask if they had seen the boys or wanted to see them. She didn't waste her time bad-mouthing them or trying to get in some bag of mix-up with them to make herself look better to me. I wondered if females understood that did not make them look better to a man. Men just wanted less drama and more emotional support, even if we didn't come out and ask for it.

Sahnai really needed to get it together. Yeah, I slipped up and slept with her a few times, and I was really regretting that shit now. It was before me and Alani were official, and after I talked some sense into Sahnai to get her head straight, I was going to tell baby girl what happened. I knew she was going to be hurt, but it would be better to be hurt from me telling her than finding out from my confused-ass baby mama. I was young, but honestly, I was trying to be a man about my shit. I saw what my pops did to my mom and how much that shit hurt her. She was walking around here all these years with a smile on her face for me and Dana, but it was all a lie. She was living just as bad as Phantom's mom, except she was woman enough to not take it out on her kids. I really needed to go to Jamaica soon and talk to my dad and tell him to let my mom go. Why hold on to someone when you were just going to treat them like shit and keep breaking their heart? I was starting to feel like I didn't know anyone around me. Dana was acting like a straight crazy person. I didn't know if she was doing drugs or just needed to be in someone's mental unit, but I had had enough. *I got enough stress of my own with just being a full-time dad.*

Shit, I didn't even have it in me to tell Phantom about this shit yet. That nigga was like a ticking time bomb, and my moms was the only mom he really ever had. *He may lose it and try to take on my pops or kill his side chick. With this dude there is no telling. Thank God he has Inaya and Kadia back because it's clear that they are where his heart is.* I still couldn't get over how Sahnai was treating Inaya. She was mad because her cousin was a good girl and not a thot like her. I didn't understand how you grew up with somebody like sisters and then treated them like the enemy. I knew now Sahnai and I were done for good. Even if Alani and I didn't work out, even if she once again became the woman I knew and loved, I couldn't go back. *Look at how I am dealing with all this shit with my family and my son being sick, and all she can think about is breaking up me and the only one I got in my corner right now.*

Seeing my phone light up with Phantom's number, I reached and answered, "Yo, son, what's good?"

"Lox, I need you to come meet me up at Strong Hospital ASAP, cuz. This some shit that you have to be here to see. Toya had her baby, man, and shit is all fucked up. Can you get down here right away?"

Hearing my cousin sound stressed like he was put me into high speed. Throwing my sweats on and a white tee, I grabbed some Nike slides and threw my feet inside. *What now? How is this shit even my problem?* I couldn't help but wonder as I ran downstairs. As soon as I thought it through, I put that shit out of my head. If Phantom needed me, I was there. He and Inaya had been there for me 100 percent helping with the kids and treating Alani good. Plus, we always had each other's backs. I was really just annoyed with a lot of other people, and I couldn't let that attitude reflect on me and my cousin.

Seeing Alani and my mom sitting at the table while she was rocking Aiden back and forth in her arms made a smile come to my face.

"Babe, I have to go to the hospital and see what's up with this nigga Phantom. He called and said Toya had her baby, and he needs me to come up there. I don't know what's wrong, but you know how it is. If he needs me, I'm there. You and the kids good though?" I asked, making my way over to kiss her before I left.

"Yeah, I am all right, babe. Q and Vivy are taking a nap, and Aiden just fell asleep. I can roll wit' you if you want. Your mom is here if she don't mind watching the kids."

"Sweetie, I don't mind. You go with him. Knowing Phantom's crazy behind, Inaya may need you. Bring back my little baby Kadia if she is up there. I am sure Vivy missed her, being stuck with all these boys," my mom said in her quiet voice.

"Okay, babe, you ready?" *I hope she doesn't have to go do any makeup or shit like that.* I didn't want to leave cuz waiting forever. I knew how these females were. Man, I remembered how long Phantom and I used to have to wait on Azia's ass back in the day. It used to take her an hour to get ready to go to the store, and don't even get me started on Sahnai's ass. It was easier to just leave her behind.

A few minutes later, Alani came walking in the room with her curly hair pulled back by a gray headband, some gray tights, a white hoodie that showed some of her belly, and some white Chuck Taylors. I thought all she did was put on shoes and kiss the kids in their sleep.

"Ready," she said with a smile. I loved how she smelled when she walked in the room. It was like the sweetest smell ever. It was that Michael Kors shit she always wore. I even bought it for her a few times. Really though, it was her essence. She made the perfume smell good. It didn't even smell the same on other females or on the little white pieces of paper they had in the mall when they did the test sprays. When my baby walked in the room, it was her. She was like honey and sunshine mixed together. Naw, fuck that. Being around her was like being home.

Not saying anything, I grabbed her hand, and we made our way to my black Benz. Once we got inside, I hopped on the 590 headed to the east side. We just listened to the music on the ride over, not saying much but not feeling like we had to either. It was comfortable. She wasn't chatting my ear off because she felt pressured or uncomfortable. I just wished we were headed somewhere fun or relaxing. I still remembered when she and I had the getaway weekend in the mountains. That shit was where it was at. Instead, we were walking into more drama. I was wondering if I should have left her home. *No telling what Toya has up her fucking sleeve.* Maybe she got a whole other baby father, or maybe she killed someone. I wouldn't be surprised at any scenario.

Hopping off at the Portland Avenue exit, I turned into the hospital and followed the signs to the garage. I grabbed the ticket and waited for the arm to go up, and then I drove through. I finally found parking on the fifth floor. I guessed the hospital was busy. Maybe it was the warm weather, probably more people out in the streets hurting each other. Walking into the elevator, I felt a feeling of dread wash over me all of the sudden. I guessed Alani could sense how I felt, because she grabbed my hand and squeezed it.

"Babes, it's gonna be all right. I am sure it's not too serious. Maybe it just turned out to be Phantom's baby and Inaya is upset. He may just need you for moral support," she offered as an explanation as to why we were here.

Shrugging my shoulders and kissing her gently on the forehead, I responded, "I guess you're right." Walking to the nurse's station, I stopped so we could get the room number and directions on how to get to the maternity ward. Being here made me feel some kind of way since I was denied the pleasure of being in the hospital to see either one of my sons born. "Hello, can we have the room for Latoya Thompson?" I asked.

"Room 314. Take the red elevators on the right, and they will let you in at the desk up there."

Before I knew it, I was standing outside of door 314. I decided to call Phantom and let him know I was here.

"Yo, where you at? I am outside of her room," I called and asked.

"Just come in. I am in here waiting on you."

Hearing his response, I hung up and pushed the door open. Phantom and Inaya were sitting in chairs next to a table, and Toya was in bed half asleep. Before I could even ask him what was going on, he motioned toward the baby's bassinet. *Damn, what is going on? Did she have twins on his ass?* Inaya looked calm, not mad or upset, so I was not sure what the fuck was happening.

Slowly looking in the tiny wooden contraption with the wheels on the bottom and drawers on the side, I saw a baby who looked identical to Aiden, except he was much smaller. It looked like his tiny baby clothes and blanket were swallowing him whole. The colorful hat the hospital put on the baby was sliding down, covering his eyes. Gently pushing the baby's hat up some so he wouldn't smother, I saw them. Shiny green eyes glared back at me, angry because I'd disturbed his sleep.

"Toya, what the fuck? I know there is no way this can be my baby. I only started fucking you again about four months ago when I came back from Jamaica, so you better start explaining this shit now." I guessed me screaming at his mom scared the baby, and he started crying at the top of his lungs. Toya rolled her eyes at me and cut her eyes at Phantom while she snatched the baby out of the little crib and tried to hush him.

Seeing the door swing open and hearing his voice was starting to seem like a bad fucking dream.

"Why is my baby crying, Toya? Please remember I will fuck you up about mi pickney dem." Stopping in his tracks, my father looked at me and then Phantom with a confused look on his face. *Why the fuck is my dad here, in the U.S., in a room filled with thot Toya and a baby he is calling his own?* Before I could even address this bullshit, I heard my own voice playing in the quiet room.

"Yes, Sahnai, fuck me just like that. I will never stop fucking this pussy. I love you so much, girl. Please come home to me and our kids."

Now all eyes were on me. I could feel them staring, burning a hole in my back and the side of my head. Lifting my head with no real enthusiasm, I looked up at Alani, who was holding her phone with silent tears streaming down her cheeks. *No, no, no. Fuck. Why did Sahnai do this? Why is she messing up the best thing in my life and our sons' lives?*

"I didn't think you would have anything else to say, Lox. This video says it all. Sorry I am not Sahnai and that I will never be Sahnai or Toya. I don't have sex with just anyone, and I would never turn my back on my kids, but I can see that's the kind of shit that makes you fall in love." With that said, Alani calmly turned around and walked out of the room.

Hearing the hospital room door close with a light thud, I didn't know what to do. I had to deal with this shit with my father, and now Alani was gone, and I thought Inaya was about to beat me with one of those metal poles they hung the IV bags on. Phantom held her tightly to him like he could read her mind, but at the same time, he was looking at my dad with those cold, dead black eyes.

"Dad, what the fuck?"

"Dad, really? You are cheating on Mom with this bitch? Oh, my God. I thought it was Sahnai. I thought little Q was Dad's baby. That is why I did everything I did. Sahnai is never going to forgive me," sobbed Dana, who flew through the door, interrupting me. Reaching out to her to calm her down, I now understood why she had been acting so mean lately. Somehow she found out about our dad having another baby with someone else.

"Hush, Dana, it's okay. Sahnai will forgive you. She will understand. She'd better. She is not always nice to people either," I told her in the most reassuring voice I could come up with.

She leaned her head against my chest. I could feel her little body shaking and her tears soaking my T-shirt. In a wobbly voice, Dana continued talking.

"Lox, you don't understand. I wasn't just mean to Sahnai. I am the one who stabbed her."

Chapter 7

Phantom

Looking at the house one last time, all I could do was shake my head. This nigga Lox was going to have a lot to deal with after my uncle dropped that bomb. *That dude ain't shit cheating on my aunt like that, and even worse, with a thot like Toya. How the fuck did those two even meet my uncle all the way in Jamaica? He barely comes to the States, let alone to mess around. I'ma see what Lox wants to do, and we can handle that situation later.*

I had to watch him walk to his Range when we left. I didn't even start my whip until he pulled off. Once he heard his pops was Toya's baby father, he started throwing tables and shit. Some medical utensils hit the bitch in her face, and her baby started wailing. Once security came, I knew it was time to go. I didn't know about him, but I was strapped and not going to prison for fighting in a maternity ward.

I was already feeling like shit running out on Inaya, but I knew that me hurting her and breaking her down would not benefit her. I hated seeing her lying there on the couch almost lifeless. I didn't know why I couldn't do right, but I just couldn't. Maybe I could for someone else, but Inaya made my heart beat, and if I got all caught up with her, then my heart would be broken when she decided to do me wrong.

I called this bitch Ashena as I sped through the streets on my way to her job. As soon as she answered her phone, I was picking her up for a ride she wouldn't forget.

"Hey, baby, how are you today? Did daddy miss me? Want me to meet you on my break outside? I will lick your balls the way you like. We don't even have to go anywhere. We can just meet in the car or the back of the building."

This was how the bitch answered the phone, no self-respect and thirsty as hell. Inaya would never say any dumb shit like that to me. She always carried herself classily, even if she didn't always stand up to me like she should have. I let this thot ruin what I had with a good girl, made it so I had to walk away from my kids full-time because she couldn't just stay in the side chick's job. *I'ma start asking for resumes in the future when I fuck with these bitches.* Thinking about that shit made my heart race with anger.

"Yo, what time you go on break, ma? I am nearby, and that shit you talking sounds good." I tried to keep my voice calm when I spoke to her. I didn't want her to hear the rage I felt.

"I can go on lunch now. Meet me in the lobby."

Pulling up in the alley next door to the gas company, I put my nine under the seat. If I took that shit in there, they were going to be scraping that bitch up from in front of her desk, and then I would be on the news in the middle of a police shootout. Pushing the doors open, I saw her standing there with a smile on her face, posted up, leaning against the desk like she was cute. Leaning in and giving her a hug, I greeted her and led the way outside.

"Bae, where you parked at, so I can show you what you missed?" she asked with a smirk on her face.

"So, Shena, you thought this shit was cute or what, fucking with my wifey, sending texts and calling?" I began shouting as I slammed her up against the building. I was trying everything not to hurt this bitch, but her face wasn't making it any easier. She had her lips turned up in some goofy-ass smile even though I knew it was getting hard for her to breathe. Dropping her to the ground, she stumbled as her black stilettos hit the grooved pavement.

"Come on, Phantom, wifey? If she were wifey, you wouldn't have been riding me around, fucking me, and letting me fuck with her head on the regular. At least I didn't tell her about our baby. I left something as a surprise for later on," she spit out, laughing so hard she was bent over, holding her sides. In true thot fashion, she didn't care how loud she was or that her coworkers were staring at her as they left the building for their own lunches. I bet this bitch was the joke of the office. I wondered how she even kept a job here.

Grabbing her by her arm, I led her to the alley near my car. Leaning up against the wall, I dropped my gray Puma sweatpants and my boxers and pushed her roughly to her knees. She never even cried out as the gravel cut into her bare skin. She just gobbled up my dick in her mouth like it was her last meal.

I made sure to fuck her mouth extra hard all while I had a huge smile on my face because I couldn't wait for what happened next. Thinking of some freaky shit I saw on a movie, I made sure to nut fast, watching her mouth open as cum ran down the sides of her chocolate cheeks. I laughed. "So, you carrying my baby, huh?" I asked with a smile. Not being able to speak, she nodded her head up and down with a glint in her eye. Snatching her by her weave, I jumped back as thick white nut flew all over. "Bitch, the only place I ever came was in your mouth, so unless you have some magic way of getting pregnant from your raggedy-ass lips, I know you're not carrying my seed." Watching the nigga in the dark blue hoody and basketballs shorts come out from behind the car, I let her go and she fell to the ground.

"Ashena, you're pregnant for real, B? Well, damn, I could have sworn you were on your period when you left home today. This the shit you do when you go to work? Got niggas nuttin' in your mouth, the mouth you kiss our kids with at night!" he yelled out in rage as he reached for her.

Feeling like my work was done, I dapped the li'l dude up and jumped in my ride, laughing. "Hey, Shena, next time you want to play a game, get a Nintendo and don't contact my woman again, because I won't spare your life in the future." She was struggling to get up, and her tears were falling, mixing with my cum that was all over her face. I wondered how she was going to explain that shit to her man. Not my fucking problem, though. I could have killed her, but I was trying to be a better man since I had a little girl now and a baby on the way.

Riding around, trying to find Cudjie, I beat my hands on the steering wheel. I didn't want to leave without handling him, but it was like this nigga disappeared into thin air. I should have taken him out the day I had the chance. I rode by his favorite hangouts, clubs, and even the gym he went to, but nothing. Grabbing one of my phones, I made one more call before I headed to the airport.

"Azia, look, I need to see Kadia before I leave. I can't just leave without seeing her. She has been through enough already." Hearing nothing but silence, I thought my sister hung up on me. "Azia, you hear me!" I shouted in the phone.

"Look, it's not a good time right now. I will call you later," she said, and then she hung up in my ear. I guessed I deserved that, but I hoped she knew I was calling right the fuck back.

Three Months Later

Sitting on the balcony, I propped my feet up on the railing and leaned back in the white wicker chair. Looking at the sunrise, I realized I felt alone. I had been in Miami for three months now. Every day seemed longer than the last. I missed Inaya and Kadia. All I did was drink, fuck randoms, and spend money. Honestly, I felt like shit most of the time. I couldn't stop thinking about the last time I saw Iny. She was lying in a hospital bed with an IV in her arm. She looked so fragile. The baby, my baby, was making her sick. Hell, maybe it was me and all my bullshit making her sick. I sat next to her, holding her hand. I could still feel the way her hand felt, like silk, so soft and comforting, but tiny and frail.

After I had called Azia back-to-back the day I left, she told me I couldn't see Kadia because Iny was in the hospital, and of course, I went to make sure she was all right. The guilt of seeing her that way, however, made me leave even faster.

I sat a while longer watching the sun come up and sipping bottled water. I had to get my head right because Lox was coming to see me today so we could handle some business. Not that I gave a fuck how he saw me, but he was bringing my baby girl, Kadia. Her mother had made shit beyond difficult for me since I left. I had to get baby girl her own iPhone so we could talk, and I had to give all Kadia's money to Lox or Azia because Inaya's hard-headed ass sent every dime back to my bank account if I gave her a thing. I even heard she moved out of the place she lived in so I wouldn't know where she was if I came back. She was frustrating me so much I felt like I was going crazy, especially since no one had found Cudjie yet. So I didn't even know for sure if my kids were safe, because he was still out there, and she was playing games.

"Phantom, you coming back in here with me soon?" whined the thick Spanish girl who had just climbed out of my bed. She stood with only a white sheet wrapped around her body. For what, I didn't know, because her breasts were still showing. Still standing in the doorway with that "come fuck me" look on her face, she snaked her tongue out, licking her lips and showing me her tongue ring. I was already tired of fucking her, and it had only been a few days.

"Look, Dora, I am good. I need you to get dressed and shit and clear on out of here. My little shorty is coming to visit, and that means it's daddy-daughter time, so I will holla at you in a week or two."

Here comes the nonsense. I could already see it. Her fists balled up and clutched the sheet, and her face twisted into a crying face. This was one of the reasons I stayed drinking. Dealing with these needy-ass girls got me hot as fuck.

"My name is Daria, not Dora, and, baby, why would you want me to leave? I should be meeting my future stepdaughter. I will get dressed, *papi,* and then I will make some breakfast for all of us. I know I am special to you, and you wouldn't want me to leave. You just meant to put on some clothes." Watching her for a few minutes running around, washing up, and throwing on clean underwear and a lace bra, I was interrupted by a knock on the door.

Who the fuck was knocking? I wasn't expecting anyone for a while. Walking to the door at the same time as Dora, I shoved the bitch to the side. "Yo, don't be fucking opening my doors and shit like you live here," I reprimanded her with my hand on the handle.

As soon as I cracked the door, it flew open. While I reached for my gun, a little person flew at me, screaming, "Daddy!" Reaching up to grab baby girl before she fell, I hugged her close. She smelled like that pink baby lotion her mom still used on her, and she looked cute as always. Her hair was in two of those pigtail things with curls and red ribbons, and her little khaki-colored dress looked nice with her Burberry slippers and a matching handbag she wore around her neck. Lifting the little purse up for closer inspection, I looked at Kadia.

"Auntie Azia," we both said at the same time. Only my sister would be buying a small child designer handbags. I guessed I should be thankful she had three boys and no girls.

"Daddy, I missed you so much. Please come home. Mommy is sad and mean without you. Daddy, she . . ." Kadia trailed off as I looked up and saw where she was staring. *Fuck.* I told this bitch to leave, and now my daughter was standing here looking at her ass in some drawers and a bra.

"Yo, what the fuck, Dora? I know I told you to leave. Why are you still standing there with no clothes on?" Putting Kades down next to me, I grabbed her ass and threw her and her shit out the front door. Hearing Lox laugh as he stepped over her body, struggling with the luggage, I picked Kadia back up and made my way to the kitchen. "Yo, Lox, can you make sure the hall is clear so I can take my princess to breakfast?" I directed, ignoring his snickers and shit.

"Kadia, what were you saying about Mommy?" I asked. I was hoping we could skip the naked woman in my living room.

"Daddy, who was the naked lady, and why was she in your house? Don't you love Mommy anymore? Is she your new girlfriend? Daddy, do you kiss her? Ew," she ended her little rant, but I was not off the hook. She stood in front of me with her hands on her hips and her head tilted to the side, waiting; looking just like her mother.

"No, she is not my 'girlfriend,' and no, I only kiss Mommy. Now let's forget about her. She was lost, and I am sure she will find her way home. Go wash your hands at the sink, and Daddy is going to take you to breakfast," I told her, gently nudging her toward the sink.

"I bet she will find her way home, Daddy. Her name is Dora, and Dora has a map and a purple backpack and always finds her way home," she shot back as she skipped to the sink.

Not even bothering to hold my laugh in once Lox laughed at Kadia, I turned back to the door. "Naw, she ain't come, so stop looking at the door like that, son. No one else is walking through it. I left the boys with Azia and just brought Kadia. I tried to get Iny to come, but these days she won't listen to a damn thing, so I left her alone before she changed her mind about Kades coming."

"Cool," I responded, nodding my head. *I guess it's for the best*. If Inaya had come and seen the naked pop off in my living room, she would have been more than hurt. She would have been pissed. I was just going to enjoy this time with my shawty.

"So that's it? Cool? You not even gonna ask how she doing?" Lox asked, staring at me with a frown on his face.

"I'm saying, son, she has a decent roof over her head, and I am sure you and my sis won't let her ass starve, so what else is there to know?" I heard him laugh, but not in the funny ha-ha way. His frown got deeper if at all possible.

"Yo, Kadia, go wait in the other room, and watch TV for a minute, and then you and Daddy can hit the road."

"Okay, Uncle Lox," my baby girl replied, quickly doing as she was told.

"Inaya is not okay. She almost lost the baby in September and spent weeks in the hospital. She cries so much all she does is get sick. She lost too much weight. It brings tears to my eyes when I see her. She is like a shell of the person she used to be, bags under her eyes and her clothes falling off her body. Son, she even moved to Ghost Town. Shit is all the way fucked up."

"What the fuck you mean she moved to Ghost Town? With Kadia and carrying my li'l one? Is she fucking crazy? How is she managing over there? I mean, Lox, shit is crazy over that way. That shit ain't safe."

Fuck, what the hell is wrong with Inaya? All she had to do was stay where she was if she didn't want to move into a house, or she could have gone with Azia or even Alani. *Why is she risking our kids' safety? This shit is just reckless as fuck.*

"When she first moved there, she went to carry groceries in the house. She carried two bags in and came back and the rest were gone, stolen in broad daylight. They break into the Audi like it's a job they're going to. I mean, this shit is on the regular, son. I take Kadia to school a lot. All Kades does is cry for you and treat Inaya like she is a wicked witch, and that makes Iny even sadder. It's time for you to come the fuck home, especially while you over here acting all outraged and shit. You want to say something, do something and come home and fight for your family. There ain't nothing here these li'l niggas Riz and Luda can't handle, so stop hiding behind business."

Standing up and grabbing my wallet off the counter and the keys to my white Mercedes S-Class, I turned to Lox one more time. "Son, I am good where I'm at. Kadia, let's go, baby."

We hurried and made it to IHOP, which was my baby's favorite spot. She chatted the whole time she ate her chocolate-chip pancakes with a ton of whipped cream on top. I was just happy she didn't choke the way she was telling me everything I missed and inhaling her food at the same time. "Daddy, my new room has a white wall, and I don't like it. It's not pretty. I want a pink wall with purple and blue hearts or stars. Ooh, Daddy, maybe both. I have a best friend in school, and her name is Lashae. She is so pretty, Daddy, and wears bright colors all the time."

While she stopped to catch her breath and drink some apple juice, I figured I would ask some questions. "I thought Vivy was your best friend. Aren't you still in the same class as her?"

Tilting her head and placing her finger on her chin, she looked just like Inaya. "Daddy, Vivy is my cousin, so she is more than a best friend. Family first, Daddy, remember you taught me that?"

I felt my heart smile if that was even a thing. I felt like Lox just brought baby girl to see me so I would come back home. Shit, it may have been working, but I didn't like anyone pulling my strings. "Come on, Kades, let's go do your favorite thing in the whole world."

Jumping out of her seat and twirling around, she shouted, "Yay, let's go shopping." And just like that, I was smiling again and so was everyone else in the restaurant. Throwing down a fifty, I grabbed her hand, and we walked out to the strip.

By three p.m., we had hit fifteen stores, and I had to make three trips to the car to drop off bags. Feeling myself being pulled into another store by Kadia, I decided to try to be the dad and set some limits or something. "Kades, look, this is the last store, all right, baby girl? I am not Auntie Azia. I can't shop more than five hours, or I will turn into a vampire and start biting people," I joked with her.

"Poor Daddy," she said, patting my hand and walking into Kids Foot Locker. I didn't think she believed me any more than I did. Picking up white and pink and white and orange Adidas, I called over the salesgirl and took a seat. I wondered if I had "baller" on my forehead. Damn, I had on some leather sandals, ripped jean shorts, and a black V-neck Armani shirt. It was a plain shirt, no logo or anything. No jewelry on except my earrings and the ice in my mouth, yet here came the salesgirl with a look of thirst in her eyes and the ho walk in her step.

"Hello, sir, how can I help you today?" she asked with a huge grin on her face. I could see all her thirty-twos, and that shit wasn't pretty at all.

"Whatever Jordans came out this month I need in a preschool size twelve and in a newborn size." She was still standing there smiling, so I looked around, wondering if I forgot something. "Oh, yeah, and bring whatever she wants in size twelve," I said, pointing to Kadia, who was patiently holding several pair of display shoes in her arms.

"Daddy, I want two of these so Vivy can have a pair too and we can wear our matching outfits to school on Monday," she said in her sweetest voice as she thrust the sparkly pink sneakers in the salesgirl's hand last. "Two pair of the sparkly ones," I told her with a smirk. Her smile quickly turned to a frown when I didn't give her whatever the hell it was she wanted from me.

Walking from the back with several boxes of shoes, she set them down in front of me. "Sir, which ones would you like?" she said, trying to bend over in her uniform khakis so I could get an ass shot.

These bitches are disgusting. Like, I am here with my fucking kid. Have some class. "I want all of them," I threw at her as I grabbed Kades's hand and walked to the register. I was excited about my and Inaya's baby, and I was happy to be buying my child something. I really didn't care if it was a boy or a girl. I just wanted to know so I could be involved, buy some shit, brag to Lox and my li'l niggas, and most of all, make sure my kid knew how much I loved him or her.

"Daddy, I think she likes you," Kadia whispered not very quietly.

"I bet she does, baby, but I only like Mommy," I replied in a not-so-quiet tone of voice while kissing her on her nose. I didn't ever want my kids to see me disrespect their mother or think another woman could take her place, because another woman never could.

Inaya

Stepping outside and seeing the fresh glass on the driveway of the parking lot, I noticed that my car window was busted again. *Fuck, I don't know why these people keep breaking into my car.* Sighing, I rubbed my round belly with one hand and turned Kadia around to go back in the house with the other. "Come on, baby, Mommy has to call the insurance company so they can come and fix the car," I explained to her, trying not to let her see the tears forming in my eyes. This meant she would be late to school again. At least I was off today. I only had class in the evening around six. Pleading with myself not to let any tears fall, I grabbed her some yogurt out of the fridge—those colorful kid-themed ones with the pink and blue swirls—and handed her a spoon.

"Mommy, I don't like it here. Why did we have to move? It's scary here, and I don't think Daddy would want us here," she said to me with her eyes wide and tears dropping off of her face.

When Phantom left, I stopped using his money. I filed for disability through my job when I was so sick I had to miss a month at work. That time was the worst for me. I didn't know a person could be that sick and still live. I ended up in the hospital, and the baby's life was in danger. All the crying I did over Phantom made it worse. I felt so guilty after I found out the baby was in distress. I decided to stop crying, and that was how I started to get better, stronger, and determined to leave these feelings for Phantom behind. I knew I had come too far to sit around crying myself a river, and now I had two kids to get it together for.

So I used my own money to move into this cheap place until after I had this baby. So now we lived in the hood, on a street called Saxton, to be exact. I had half a house with two bedrooms. The place was well maintained, but I had to deal with gunshots all day and night, people breaking into my car—yeah, I kept his Audi—weekly, and the normal crackheads and bums who came with the hood. And then there were the next-door neighbors. They were a whole other story with the fighting, screaming kids all day and night and all the banging on the walls. I was now four and a half months pregnant, and this had become my life. I went back to work a few weeks ago, part-time, and I was still slowly making my way through my final semester of school.

Hanging up with the insurance company, I decided to get my hormones in check and call Lox to see if he could take Kadia to school. Now that we moved, she still went to her private school. They just refused to bus her where we lived. Phantom took care of her tuition from wherever he was and made sure that Lox or his sister came by and took her shopping once every other week or so. Azia always tried to spend some of the money on me when we went places or she bought stuff. She was still my best friend, and we still considered ourselves sisters. I saw her every week, and we talked on the phone daily. One thing I loved about Azia was that she never offered an opinion on my and her brother's situation or on the decisions I made even when she didn't agree with them all.

Now, Kadia, she came home with all kinds of stuff— toys, clothes, and even food—when she went with her aunt or uncle. I mean, damn, I got food stamps, so I wasn't sure what that was all about, but what the fuck ever. Phantom always was an asshole, so I was sure it was his doing. When Kadia talked to Phantom, he never asked to speak to me or even asked how I was doing. I was sure his family kept him updated anyway, or he just really didn't care. Just a few weeks ago, I let Lox take her to see Phantom in, well, wherever the hell he was. I was assuming Florida because my baby came back with summer clothes in the fall, Disney stuff, and a tan. I was still not sure sending her was the best idea. Ever since she had gone, it was Daddy this and Daddy that, and her attitude had been on a hundred.

Hearing the phone pick up and Lox saying hello, I quickly said, "Hello," before he hung up.

"What's up, li'l sis? You and the kids good?" he asked. I really didn't want to tell him about the car because he was going to lecture me about the thousands of dollars I had my bank reject and send back weekly and how we didn't have to live like this.

"Lox, they broke into the car again, and now I have to wait on the insurance company. I am not asking for money or anything—I have the deductible on my card—I just need you to take Kadia to school, please?" Hearing him pause and sigh, I knew he was pissed.

"Okay, Inaya. I am on my way," he said in an even tone as he hung up. I guessed he had given up on lecturing me at least.

"Uncle Lox is coming to get you for school, so you don't have to cry, baby," I said while stroking her long hair. She decided to wear it out this year with just a headband or in ponytails with curls. No barrettes or beads for right now.

"Good. I want to go live with Uncle Lox. I hate it here, and I hate you!" she screamed, running to stand next to the front door. Her arms were crossed, and her little body was shaking from crying. Looking down at my shaking hands, I took a few deep breaths and walked to the front and waited with her. She had had these outbursts a lot since Phantom had been gone and more since her visit with him.

Feeling my phone vibrate, I thought it was Lox calling to say he was outside, but it was a bunch of messages from Marvin.

Marvin: Hey, baby, what are you doing?

Marvin: I want to take you to breakfast, beautiful.

Marvin: Are you kid-free?

I wished he would get an iPhone. That could have all been one message. Deciding I was hungry, I responded that we should meet at Cracker Barrel in two hours. I was hoping to have a rental or a fixed car by then. Marvin was a guy I met a while ago at school. He was always trying to holla at me even before I met Phantom, but I always brushed him off. Two months ago, I had to work on a research paper, and he was assigned as my partner. Somewhere along the way of him constantly pursuing me and annoying me, we got close and became friends. I mean, just friends. I was pregnant and had a kid. I wouldn't be bringing random men around my kids. I kept telling Marvin that I couldn't be serious with him right now. Maybe someday. He was a nice guy with a steady job. He was a personal trainer in a private gym downtown. Sometimes his healthy ways really got under my skin. Like, I was pregnant. If I wanted doughnuts with sprinkles and frosting, so the fuck what? But Marvin made sure to tell me how I should be eating sugarless, wheatless, tasteless snacks instead.

Hearing Lox outside, Kadia ran out without so much as a backward glance and threw her arms around Lox like I was beating her or something. "Iny, I will pick her up today from school and keep her for the weekend. I have a surprise for her," he said while Kadia danced around in delight.

"Lox, don't bring any more toys in my damn house," I said with a serious-ass face. I felt like FAO Schwarz and Toys "R" Us got married and had toy babies in my house.

As he flipped me the bird behind her back and drove away, the insurance people rolled up. "Ma'am, we will have this fixed and vacuumed for you in about an hour," the repairman stated.

"Thank you, Mike," I responded. Poor Mike had been to my house five times this month. Shaking my head, I wobbled myself into the house and upstairs to get dressed. Finding some leggings that were all gray and a white and gray striped sweater, sliding my feet into gray Ugg slippers—shoes were a struggle these days with the baby bump and swollen feet—I walked downstairs and had a small snack of an apple and some hot chips while I waited to leave. This baby had me craving all kinds of shit. I'd been eating peaches and ranch, gummy worms on my ice cream, and peanut butter everything, and I hate peanut butter normally.

Once I made it inside my Audi—I mean, Phantom's Audi—I sank down in the seat and thought about him. This car always reminded me of him. Maybe that was why I loved it so much. It was the only thing I allowed myself to keep that he gave me. I knew this seemed fucked up. I mean, yeah, I was talking to Marvin casually. He was kind of a rebound, I guessed, because my heart still missed Phantom. But what the fuck could I do? He left me. I didn't leave him. I sat back and took him the way he was, loved him unconditionally, even when he hurt me. I knew if I fussed at him and told him to stop cheating on me, he was going to leave. I didn't count on him leaving anyway. I never knew he cared that he was hurting me, and I didn't know that leaving your pregnant girlfriend was showing her you cared.

Pulling out into traffic, I jumped on the 390 West toward Henrietta. Pulling beside Marvin's 2016 Jeep in the restaurant parking lot, I threw my shades on and looked around, wondering how I even made it here because I was driving and not paying attention to where I was going, just thinking about Phantom. Noticing Marvin standing at the door, I walked over and snaked my arm through his. Walking to the door, I tried to listen to some story he was telling me. *Shit, I have no clue what the story was about.* Suddenly, I felt a tingle run through my body. That was when I looked up just in time to stop myself from running into Phantom.

"Hey, Iny, you're looking good, ma," he said as he leaned down and kissed me on my cheek. He let his hand roam to my belly, lightly touching the bump where his baby was.

I trembled a little, and our baby began jumping around like he or she knew their daddy was nearby. I could feel Marvin tense up as I snatched my arm out of his in a guilty motion. I could feel my skin begin to burn, and without even trying, I stood there looking Phantom up and down. He looked better than I could remember. No picture did him justice. His hair was in fresh braids going straight to the back, and he had on some straight blue jeans with a few rips on the legs. His feet had Burberry sneakers on them, and he had a khaki-colored jacket that matched. I could smell the scent of his Armani cologne lingering from his hug.

"Yo, Iny, you good, ma? My baby good? You look like you need some water or a seat or something," he said when I still hadn't said anything, and I could hear the laughter in his voice.

I tried to pull myself together and brush off this guilty feeling. I mean, what the fuck was I guilty of? This dude walked out on me. He left without a phone call or a note—nothing. I knew my limits, and Marvin was just a friend until I was in a position to take it further.

"Phantom, I am fine, and the baby is fine. I am assuming that you are Kadia's surprise from Lox. She will be really happy to see you. I will pick her up later on because she has school in the morning."

"So you not gonna introduce me to your friend or nothing? Oh, and, Inaya, I will bring my daughter back when I feel like it. I know the way to her school, so she is Gucci," he said with his normal mean-ass smirk on his face.

"Marvin, this is my baby's father, Phantom. Phantom, this is my friend Marvin. There, now you are introduced and excused. I have your baby to feed. Have a nice day, Phantom, and let me know when I can pick up our child." With that said, I grabbed Marvin's hand and walked toward the hostess stand.

Chapter 8

Phantom

Being back in the Roc had been good. I was still trying to find Cudjie, but so far he had stayed under the radar, and that was pissing me off. Being home with my daughter had made me more than happy, and I was glad to be closer to Inaya, even though I had still decided that I was not the one for her. She seemed happy with that Marvin dude anyway, and who was I to interrupt that? Although when I saw her and ol' boy at the restaurant, I wanted to snap his neck then throw Inaya over my shoulder and hide her away in a secret room somewhere. I was sure my thoughts sounded like a crazy person or some stalker baby daddy type shit, but it was what it was.

I had been staying at my sister's house since it made no sense to stay alone. Lying in the guest room, listening to the kids giggle and play, I knew I had been in this house too much lately. Picking up the bottle of Cîroc from the bedside table and drinking was something I had been doing too much of lately. I decided I needed to go out. Picking up the phone, I called Lox. "Yo, nigga, what's up? Let's hit up that new spot downtown. Empire, I think it's called. My boy Von is having a party tonight." Waiting for a response, I figured he was going to have some excuse because this dude had spent all this time trying to win Alani back, and li'l sis was still not budging. She still let him see Vivy and would hang out with the girls, but aside from that, she ignored him.

"A'ight, pick me up at eleven," he said before hanging up in my ear. He was one of those people who never said "later" or anything. Just a dial tone when he was done talking. *Rude-ass nigga,* I thought before I threw the cell down on my bed.

Wandering into the living room, I saw Azia hanging up her phone as soon as she saw me. "I know it was Iny. What is she doing? My kids okay?" Rolling her eyes, she started watching the TV again, turning up the volume. Snatching the remote out of her hand and throwing myself on the couch next to her, I decided that she was going to talk to me today. Since I left Inaya, my own sister barely spoke to me.

"Azia, I am your brother. I shouldn't have to remind you of how I have always had your back, always been there for you. Inaya is not your sister, so that means you need to be on my side, so when I ask you a question, you should open up that pretty mouth and answer me." Flicking her on her lip, I watched her face turn up into a frown, and her tiny arms suddenly crossed.

"Inaya is my sister now, and I am not talking to you because I am mad at you. I love you and appreciate you, but I am mad at you. Why can't you let go of all the stuff from the past? I know Mommy was fucked up and Dad too. They didn't love me either. They lied to me and mistreated me. My husband left me. He died doing a job I begged him to quit, and how he thought I would manage alone with three kids is beyond me. But I never let those things break me or ruin my heart. I know someday I will love again, and I will be willing to trust the man I am with and give him a chance. Why couldn't you just trust Iny? She is the one for you, and you are ruining any chance you have. But to answer your question, the kids are fine and Inaya is . . . well, she is hurting."

My sister ran up the stairs and left me sitting there wishing I had brought the bottle of Cîroc with me for this conversation. "And don't be flicking me anymore. That shit hurts. Now I want a new pair of shoes and a matching bag!" she yelled down the stairs.

Laughing to myself at the spoiled monster I helped create, I made my way upstairs to go get ready for the club. Looking in the closet at all the clothes, it made me remember how Iny's closet looked. Hell, mine too after she came over to the townhouse. The clothes were in order, color coordinated and shit, and she would lay out my outfits when we would go places. I missed that. I missed feeling loved by somebody, being loved by her. She still wouldn't speak to me. I mean, I didn't try much, but I called when I wanted Kades, hoping to hear her voice, and she just handed my baby the phone or got on the phone and mumbled okay, yes, or no like she was being forced to speak to me, so I just let it go, let her drift further away.

Grabbing some all-black jeans and a white Kenneth Cole shirt and throwing them over the chair in my room, I hopped in the shower and let the hot water run over my back. All I could think about was my girl and how cute she looked the last time I saw her. *Yeah, I'ma find a piece of ass tonight because thinking about a girl I can't be with is truly messing with my heads—the big and little one.* Once I had my clothes on, I threw a Yankee fitted on and some white sneakers from Aldo. Grabbing my phone, I saw a few messages from this girl I'd been messing with named Tamia. Tamia was a chick I met a few weeks ago when I went to the car wash. She was standing outside of a silver Infinity truck on her tiptoes, holding a little white towel in one hand, trying to wipe the water off the top of the truck.

There was something about her standing there in tight blue jeans and a bright yellow sweater. Her little ass was poking out, and every time she reached up, I could see a tattoo of red roses on her back. I was looking over the wax job I paid to have done on the Range Rover, and my gaze just happened to meet hers. I couldn't help but laugh at her struggling to reach the top.

"Ma, what are you, five feet two or three? You not reaching the top of the truck. Here, let me help you," I said as I grabbed the towel and easily wiped the spots away. She thanked me and we talked for about twenty minutes until we both realized it was too chilly to be standing around outside and shit.

I found out Tamia worked as a manager at Bank of America downtown and she was 21 with no kids. Tamia was a cute girl, chocolate skin tone, body was a ten, and her smile was highlighted by two deep dimples on either cheek. Her wavy black hair kept blowing in her face, and she had to reach up every few minutes to brush it back. We exchanged numbers, and to be honest, I thought Tamia had been good for me. I was not in love with her. She was no Inaya, but I was enjoying her company, and I was enjoying getting to know a girl, taking it slow. We went to movies or dinner, sometimes just Netflix and chill.

Looking at her text asking me what I was up to, I decided to invite her to the club tonight so we could chill. I liked that she was not clingy, and she also didn't ask me for money since she made her own. Spraying my Dolce & Gabbana cologne on, I grabbed the keys to my Range and ran down the stairs and out the door. Driving to Saint Paul Street, I turned the radio on, and some song Iny used to always listen to came on. Listening to Beyoncé sing about her broken heart, I couldn't take my mind off the girl whose heart I knew I broke.

Can't you see there's no other man above you?
What a wicked way to treat the girl that loves you.

Damn, what a wicked way I behaved to the girl who loved me. Pulling up to the valet in front of the club, I jumped out and handed him my keys and a $100 bill.

"Yo, don't scratch my shit, and don't even try no fucking joyriding. I watch every mile," I shot back as I strolled to the VIP. Passing everyone in line, I made my way to the red rope being held up for me.

"Baby, let me come in with you."

"Daddy, I will suck your dick later," was all I heard from these thirsty bitches as I walked by. Some of them had their hands rubbing my dick, and one even grabbed my arm.

Glaring at her, I put her ass in check. "Bitch, don't be fucking grabbing me."

I wasn't even getting Tamia in this motherfucker with me. She had to stand in line like everybody else. We were casually dating, and surprisingly, I hadn't fucked anyone since me and her had been talking, but we were not a couple. I only ever really checked for one girl, and that was Inaya, and if she weren't pregnant and wanted to come out, then she would be walking in this bitch next to me. Seeing Lox already at the table, I told the waitress to bring me two bottles of Patrón, and I sat back to relax. Not really saying much, we just sat down and drank. Lox looked like he was turned up, but I was looking around the club to make sure no one was on no bullshit. We had a lot of enemies, including my brother, so I was always on the lookout for motherfuckers who wanted to catch us slipping.

Seeing Tamia looking around, I invited her and her homegirl to hang with us at our table. I could tell she was excited but trying not to show it. I was happy she wasn't acting like a basic bitch, but her friend may have been another story. Tamia was dressed cute in a little light brown sleeveless sweater-looking dress that was short as hell, showing off her thick legs with some cute short boots that matched. She had in some gold hoops, not too big, and her hair was in a wavy style and hanging past her shoulders. Standing up and giving her a hug, I grabbed her hand and pulled her to sit next to me. "Tamia, this is my cousin, Lox. Lox, this is the girl I was telling you about, Tamia."

"Hi, Lox, nice to meet you. This is my friend Rose," she said in response. Lox didn't really say much, just nodded his head at Tamia. I guessed he was not ready to see me with anyone but Inaya, but he was going to have to get past that shit. I was surprised because Lox was usually Mr. Fucking Casanova and I was the rude one.

After a lot more drinks, the night was starting to go well. Shit, Lox was even dancing with her friend. I guessed he had too much to drink, because even though she was a cute little light-skinned chick with long honey blond hair, she had some thot ways. The minute she walked in VIP, she was jumping up and down and taking selfies while holding one of the bottles. A few minutes ago, she was bent over with the little black miniskirt she had on, shaking her panty-less ass all over my cousin's $300 jeans. Anybody within ten feet could see her hairy-ass pussy out for the world to see. Taking another shot of Patrón, I let my eyes sweep the room one more time and that was when I saw someone who looked just like Azia walk through the front door of the club. Before I could look again, she and Alani were slowly walking across the VIP area until they were standing right in front of us.

Fuck, seeing the look on the girls' faces, I could tell some shit was about to go down. "So this is what y'all nasty niggas do the minute your relationship has a little problem? Wait, problems that the two of you caused. You run out here and find some new hoes to occupy your time?" Azia was doing all the talking, but I could see Alani, and the look that she had in her eyes meant that Lox should probably run or something. I had never been so happy that Inaya was pregnant and not out and about in any club. Alani calmly poured herself a drink from our table while Lox's new friend Rose started talking shit about who Azia was calling a ho. I gave her a look that said she better shut the fuck up because no matter what, Azia was my sister, and I would whoop both these girls' asses about her.

"Tamia, this is my sister, Azia, and my cousin's wife, Alani. Azia is just—"

And that was when I saw her. At almost five months pregnant, she was glowing in her light pink dress with a slit up the side. She had a jean jacket on over the dress and some jean-looking flats on. Her hair was braided back in those goddess braids and looked tight as hell. I looked down and realized I was holding Tamia's hand, and I quickly dropped it like I was handling fire. And there it was, the defeated, hurt look in her eyes. I felt my chest tighten and my hands clench at my sides. "And, Tamia, this is my children's mother, Inaya."

Inaya said a quiet, "Hello," and then turned to Lox. She basically shoved Rose out of the way and gave Lox a big hug. He never looked back at Rose as he made sure Inaya had water and was comfortable. I guessed when it came to some things Inaya didn't give a fuck about hurting bitches' feelings, just not when it came to me. Walking back to me as the girls sat at the table across from us, Lox just shook his head.

"Li'l sis is good. Son, I think Alani is going to shoot me. Just watch my back because I know how she is. She all calm now, but her eyes look wild and crazy."

I sat down and had a few more drinks. Tamia didn't seem fazed by the fact that my pregnant ex-girlfriend was in the club. She sat down next to me and began sipping on her mixed drink with a smile on her face.

"I didn't know you had kids, Phantom. How many kids do you have?" she asked in an even tone.

"I have a daughter named Kades and a baby on the way. My first child died as a baby. I don't talk about it, though." I made sure to close the topic of my kids down as fast as possible. It still hurt my soul when I thought about my baby girl dying alone without me to protect her.

Nodding her head as if she were talking herself into something, she looked at me and smiled. "Two kids, huh? That is not so bad. Why are you not with their mother anymore? Seems like a fresh breakup since her belly is big," she said, staring at Inaya across the room.

"First of all, I like you. You a laidback girl, and I appreciate that. You got your head together and seem drama free. But don't be staring at my baby's mom like that, ever. I know you have heard about me in the streets, and you don't want to see that side of me. Inaya is not a mixed-up girl. She is a good girl. We are not together anymore because I couldn't stop breaking her heart, so I left. She will always be number one in my life, so if she calls, I am there. Ma is the only one with my kids, and I won't ever turn my back on my kids or her. So if you can't deal with the situation, step off. I will respect that choice a hunnit."

Grabbing my hand, Tamia pulled me up and placed my hand on her ass, then she whispered in my ear, "Meet me at my crib. I will text you the address." I could feel my dick get rock hard feeling her soft body next to mine.

That was, until I looked up and caught Inaya watching me. One tear rolled down her face before she got up. I could tell she was leaving because she grabbed her handbag and keys off the table. Seeing the flash of the Audi sign in the club lights, I smiled slightly. She kept that car, though. She really loved the Audi for whatever reason. Sighing, I signaled to Lox it was time to go.

Walking down the stairs, I wanted to run and catch up with Inaya, make sure she was okay or just be in her presence for a moment, but I realized that wouldn't be a good idea. She probably thought I was going to curse her out for coming to the club while being pregnant. I mean, I knew how Iny was, and she was not going to drink or be in a crowd while carrying the baby, so I really didn't mind. Waiting on my truck, I was happy to see the girls get in Azia's Porsche and pull off. Making my way to Tamia's crib out in Greece, I could feel my head spinning from drinking all day.

As soon as she opened the door, I was pulling her robe open and fondling her breasts. I could tell in that little bit of time she had showered because she smelled like strawberries and her hair was a little wet. My finger made its way closer to her honey pot, brushing against the black silk panties she had on. I felt her push me back a little, and her face was frowned up. "So, you just walk in, ready to fuck? No 'Hey, babe'? No 'Let's go to the bedroom,' or 'Can I rub your back'? Nothing?"

"Look, ma, this is who I am. I've been drinking, you been rubbing your sexy body all over me in the club and rubbin' on my man all night, so yeah, let's fuck. I am not a sweet, ass-kissing and making love kinda nigga. Again, if you not fucking with the kid, I can step." Before I had the last words out of my mouth, she was on her knees with my dick deep down her tight throat. "Fuck yeah, you sucking that dick so good. Don't stop, Tamia." She started playing with her pussy and flicking her nipples. Deciding I was too drunk to play games, I grabbed her hair and pulled her up. Backing her up against the kitchen counter, I pulled the black panties to the side as I grabbed a condom from my back pocket.

"Phantom, I am on the shot, baby, so you don't need that," Tamia said in my ear.

"Hey, girl, the shot doesn't protect from diseases," I told her as I rammed my dick inside of her soaking wet pussy with the condom on.

Seeing her open her mouth to say something else, I used my finger to rub her clit, and then I placed it in her mouth for her to taste herself. That shit turned me on, and I could feel my man ready to bust. As a precaution, I pulled out and came on her stomach.

"Yo, ma, where is the bathroom?" I asked.

She pointed to a door off the kitchen in response. She was still leaning up against the counter, trying to catch her breath from the fuck I just gave her, and couldn't find her voice.

As soon as I flushed the toilet, I could feel my phone vibrate. I figured it was this nigga Lox, so I just ignored it and went to find a place to rest my head or something. All this liquor was starting to catch up to a nigga.

"Babe, come upstairs and relax with me. I will rub your back. You look stressed," Tamia said while grabbing my hand and pulling me upstairs with her.

Opening the door to her room, I was happy to see it was clean. Taking my phones out of my pocket and sliding my pants off, I threw myself across her brown and blue comforter and sighed as my phone rang again. As soon as that one stopped, my business phone started to buzz. Feeling soft hands run under my shirt and on to my back, I began to relax. Dozing off a little, I felt the phone vibrate again next to my hand, so I opened one eye, peeking to see who was calling me this time of the night. Seeing the picture of Inaya and Kadia flash across the screen, I woke up fast.

Feeling like someone threw a bucket of cold water on me, I jumped up, damn near tossing Tamia off of me. I answered the phone. "What's wrong, ma? You and the baby good?" I rushed and asked. Hearing Alani's voice instead of Inaya's made me hop off the bed and grab my pants from the floor because I knew something had to be wrong.

"Phantom, you need to get over here. Inaya was hurt when her house was robbed tonight. She says she is okay, but I don't want to leave her here alone, and she is refusing to stay somewhere else tonight."

I was already headed down the stairs when I told her I was on my way.

"Tee, I am out, come lock up!" I shouted up the stairs without even a backward glance. Happy she didn't make a peep, I jumped in my ride and hurried to the address I already had locked in for Inaya. I knew where she was at the moment I hit town. I just let her hardheaded ass believe otherwise.

Pulling in front of the place, I could see crackheads standing outside her front door like they were waiting for her to leave so they could have a free-for-all in my shorty's crib. I lifted up my shirt and showed these punks my nine, and they all scattered like roaches into the night. I ran up the stairs and banged on the door, and Alani flung it open. As I stepped inside, I could hear Inaya crying and see her shaking. Seeing her like this was too much for me. Picking her up, I sat her right in my lap and let her lay her head on my chest. I could feel her body jerking and her heart racing from the adrenaline she had pumping through her.

"Hush, it's okay," I murmured, rocking her back and forth. Looking around the room at the damage and then at Lox and Alani standing there, I knew I had to get my kids out of this place someway, somehow.

"Lox, call one of these young niggas over here to come secure the place until tomorrow. I am taking Inaya back to Azia's with me. She doesn't need to stay here with the place fucked up and no damn door."

Grabbing the bag Alani set next to us with what must have been Iny's clothes and shit, I walked her to the door. She didn't even fight me like I thought she would. She just stood closer to me in the cold night air. She still had on her dress and jean jacket from the club. I buckled her in like she was a small child and wrapped one of my hoodies around her. Getting in, I began to drive, and I felt her hand creep into mine. She was holding on so tight I knew she was scared. It hurt my soul seeing her like this, knowing things could be different. Maybe if I hadn't cheated and hurt her, then she would be somewhere safe.

I carried her as carefully as I could into the house and up the stairs. Taking off her clothes, I could see a few spots of blood on her little pink dress.

"Iny, are you hurt? You want to go to the hospital?" I asked in a concerned tone.

Shaking her head no, she grabbed the T-shirt I wore earlier while relaxing in the house and put it on, throwing her dirty clothes in my hamper.

"Just tell me what happened," I asked her as I began stripping out of my clothes. Remembering my little fuck session from Tamia's house, I decided to take a fast shower. Once I got out and grabbed clean boxers and a wife beater, I noticed Inaya waiting up like she always did.

"Honestly, Jahdair, I don't know what happened. I was getting out of the car and walked to the door, and then I was inside safe, or so I thought. I didn't feel like anyone was watching me as I walked to the door. Once I was inside, I went to the kitchen and started making a peanut butter and jelly sandwich on toast, and I heard a knock on the door. I just ignored it because, in that area, some random is always knocking on the door even in the middle of the night, and they are mostly begging for a few dollars or asking to borrow some dumb shit like sugar. Who the fuck is repaying you a cup of sugar?

"I sat down to eat in the living room, and the front door flew in. I didn't scream, but I almost peed myself. Two guys came in and grabbed the TV when they noticed me sitting there. While the tall one went to look in the kitchen—I think he was looking for my purse—the short one grabbed my braids and told me to give him my jewelry. I wasn't going to give up my shit without a fight, so I grabbed the orange vase and smashed him in the head. His head started to bleed, and it got on me, and he was pissed and punched me in the face. By then, I was screaming, and the next-door neighbor showed up at my door, holding the phone with the police on speakerphone. They got scared when they heard the cops on the line, and both ran past my neighbor, knocking the white lady to the ground, and that was it. It all happened so fast, and I thank God for my neighbor, even though her kids are loud as hell and her man loves whooping her ass. Hell, she saved my life, because there's no telling what else would have happened. Oh, yeah, one of them broke my TV when he turned to run by tripping over it. Kadia is going to be disappointed she won't be able to watch it in the living room anymore."

Slowly making my way onto the bed next to her, I pulled her down and wrapped my arms around her. "Ma, you should have given him the fucking jewelry or whatever he wanted. There is no replacing you. You and our baby are not replaceable, but that jewelry bullshit is. I would have bought you new shit, and you know it, and you know I will replace the TV." I felt her nod her head and then snuggle her body closer to mine. I rubbed her back and tried to fall asleep, missing this closeness, missing her, but sleep wouldn't come because I knew tomorrow I would have to deal with this robbery shit first thing.

I decided to let her have her space, so I covered her up and went to sit in the family room to watch some shit on YouTube. Turning on the latest episode of *Respect Life,* I grabbed the bottle of Grey Goose from the bar, but then thought better of it and picked up water instead. I didn't want to be one of those dads who had a problem, so I needed to slow down.

Two Days Later

As soon as she pulled up in the driveway, I watched her for a few seconds before I hopped out of my truck and grabbed my Polo duffel bag. I dared a pussy to break in my shit while I was here. I was running out of this bitch killing everything that moved. Inaya slowly scooted out of the car and then reached in the back seat, finally emerging with two grocery bags, a laptop bag, and an Aldo purse the size of a suitcase. She wobbled to the stairs. I followed right behind her. I guessed she thought if she didn't say shit to me, I would just go away. Looking at the walkway littered with empty crack bags, weed bags, and even used condoms, I could feel myself getting more pissed off than I was when I got here. Glancing up just in time to see Inaya stumble and almost fall backward down the cracked and broken stairs, I hurried and put my arms up to catch her.

Snatching away, she turned and glared at me. "Jahdair, what the fuck are you even doing here? I never invited you over to my home or asked you to come over here. Shit, Kadia is not even here. She is at your damn house, yet here you are. I hope you didn't leave our child with your new girlfriend, even though I know you're not crazy," she spat as she put her key in the door.

Snatching the bags out of her hand and closing the door behind her, I turned the shiny gold locks on the brand-new door. No evidence of the break-in existed. Man, I fucking wished she would just move. Shit, she didn't even have to live with me. I would cop shawty a place wherever she wanted, or she could just go to Azia's new crib. That was where Kadia was now. I was not even at the townhouse anymore. I had a house built next door to my sister's. It was finished a month ago, but I hadn't had the heart to furnish it or do shit else in there. I had a bed with sheets and blankets, toiletries, my clothes, and a TV. Aside from that stuff, I owned a five-bedroom, six-bathroom house that was empty, and I couldn't have baby girl staying in an empty house, so she was chilling at her auntie's crib. I guessed I was waiting for Iny to come put her personal touch on the place. Shit, she could have the house as long as it meant my kids were straight. I could grab a condo or just stay with my sister.

Seeing her turn toward me again, I was expecting to get cursed at, but instead, she took the bags from me and walked toward the kitchen with her shoulders slumped. Throwing my bag on the couch, I took off my shoes, because even in the hood, Inaya's place was spotless, and I knew she would get on me for walking in her shit with shoes on. Looking in the living room, I saw the new Samsung smart TV was sitting on the wall and there was no more broken glass. It was like a robbery never even took place, but I knew better.

I slowly followed her to the kitchen, looking at the picture frames on the walls as I went. I didn't take a look around the last time I was here, so now I was being nosy. Iny had printed out flicks of me, her, and Kadia together, and put them up on the walls. I stopped and put my hand up to the one nearest to the doorway. It was taken on the beach. That was one of the last days we spent together as a family before I fucked up again. The sun was going down, and Kadia was in my arms, asleep. Inaya was next to me with her hand on my bare chest and her head right next to my heart. She was my heart, and now she was no longer mine. That shit had a nigga feeling empty inside.

Looking up and seeing Inaya watching me, I got lost looking in her brown eyes. They seemed like they were swimming inside of her tears. She always was a big ol' crybaby. Before I could reach out to comfort her, she turned and walked away. I decided it was best if I didn't say anything. Watching her take off her fuzzy pink sweater, I was in awe of her belly. I never paid attention to Shawnie when she was pregnant because I was in the streets working on a come-up, and honestly, Shawnie just wasn't someone I gave a fuck about. Seeing Inaya with her belly poking out through her gray undershirt did something to me. I couldn't help but walk over to her. I felt like she had a spell on me.

The closer I got, the more I could tell she was tired. She had bags under her eyes, and her body was slumped over like it was too much effort to stand up straight. I hated that she worked all day and then went to class. She should have been relaxing or shopping with my sister, or lying upstairs with nothing on, waiting for me to come fuck that pregnant pussy. Leaning closer, I grabbed her arms as I kissed her lips. I wrapped my arms around her, held her close, and I felt her body relax as I ran my hands up and down her back. Even though she was on the road all day, she still smelled like her fruity perfume. Feeling movement on my belly, I realized our baby was kicking. Pulling back, Inaya grabbed my hand and placed it up against her stomach. Feeling hot tears hit my hand, I moved away and went to sit at the kitchen table.

I just sat watching Inaya move around the kitchen. It felt like old times, except she wasn't singing to me or joking around about something. The smile and laughter were missing, and all that was left was sadness and regret. Hearing my stomach growl as I smelled the food, I realized she was making my favorite: curried chicken and rice and peas. Setting the plate down in front of me, she took her food upstairs and left me with my thoughts.

This became our routine every night. I would sleep on the couch so I could be downstairs in case someone tried to break in again. I would listen to her cry out at night, but when I would make it to her bedroom, she would be fast asleep, tossing and turning, hugging her pillow. Last night, she broke me down when I covered her up. As I pulled the blanket around her shoulders, she called out my name in her sleep. "Jahdair, please don't leave me again." I lifted the covers and slid my body next to hers. I could feel her warmth as I moved closer, pulling her body into mine. I let my hand rest on her belly so I could be closer to our baby, and I fell asleep. She didn't cry out the rest of the night, and I got the best sleep I had had since I walked away from her.

Hearing both of my phones buzzing back-to-back woke me up. They must have woken Iny up too, because she began to strain against my arms. I knew it was Tamia. I forgot to call her back last night. I really liked her and was trying my best to be a good boyfriend for the first time. I figured since Inaya moved on, I should too.

"Jah, let me go. I am sure you have to get that, and I should eat something so I don't get morning sickness."

Rolling her over to face me, I laughed as her little hands were shoving at my chest, trying her hardest to push me off. "Chill, ma. I am just spending a little time with my baby. I will let you get up in a few, and you can cook me some breakfast." She settled down and let her eyes close again. I knew her ass wasn't getting enough rest. *She'd better not be stressing my baby out.*

Inaya

Having Phantom here was such a distraction. He looked good, smelled good, and made me want to rip his clothes off, throw him on the floor, and ride his dick. Since I had been pregnant, all I thought about was food, sleep, and sex, and since Phantom had been gone, I was definitely in need of sex or some kind of release. He walked into the bathroom to answer his phone, and he tried to talk quietly, but I could hear him.

"Hey, babe. I am coming to the house soon."

I guessed Tamia wasn't feeling him staying every night at my house, because if I didn't know better, I would think Jahdair, Mr. Badass, was explaining himself to a female. *Too bad the female is not me.*

"Look, Tamia, I care about you, and I respect you, but this is my family, and my children will always come first. Yeah, that means my baby moms too, especially since my baby is in her belly. I will get there soon. Make me some food or something useful instead of stressing me out." Ending the call, he washed his face and walked toward me.

"Inaya, I am about to go. My girl is not feeling this situation. If you would just move, I wouldn't have to be in your fucking space all the time, but you wanna be hardheaded, so I'ma be here later tonight." Holding me close for a second, he was gone as fast as he came.

Sitting at the kitchen table, I began to enjoy the silence until I heard Amy, the girl upstairs, start screaming at her kids. It was too early for this, especially if you knew what came next. Then her Nazi-looking-ass boyfriend was going to start stomping his feet on the floors and yelling at everyone. Once no one responded to that, his fists would come out to play. Amy would be begging for her life, and the kids would run to play somewhere outside. Except the baby. He would scream until his mother was well enough to come and care for him. Listening to this cycle would break my heart every time. I knew I should move wherever Phantom wanted me to or in with Azia or Lox or anywhere but here. I just didn't want to depend on anyone. People had never really been there for me 100 percent. I mean, sometimes people showed me they were there for me, but then when I turned around, they switched up. I was not going through that again.

Taking out my phone, I dialed the hospital to make an ultrasound appointment. I could have had one two weeks ago, but I had been putting it off. I thought subconsciously I wanted Phantom to be around when I went.

After I had my appointment booked for two days later, I decided to call Sahnai. I had been calling her for months, and her phone just went straight to voicemail. Lox thought she ran off with some man, but I felt like something was wrong. I mean, Sahnai was a hothead, and I knew Lox was pissed at her, but she had not even checked on her son, and that wasn't like her. Hearing the voicemail click on, I sighed when it stated her voicemail was full and I could not leave a message. Dialing Phantom, I waited for him to answer, listening to the phone ring in my ear.

"What's wrong, Iny? You good, ma?" he answered, sounding out of breath.

Before I could speak, I heard his bitch in the background. "So you just left her needy ass, and then she is calling you as soon as you get here? Oh, and you dumb motherfucker answers the phone while we are fucking?" She was pushing her luck talking to Phantom that way. *She will learn.*

"Anyway, baby daddy, I was calling to tell you we have an ultrasound appointment for the baby Wednesday at eight a.m. at Strong Hospital. See you then." Hanging up, I could hear Tamia screaming for Phantom to stop doing whatever it was he was doing to her. Laughing to myself, I made my way downstairs to find a snack.

Chapter 9

Alani

Lying on my leather couch, I could feel my bare skin sticking to the cushions. It was cool outside, but with the heat on, I began to sweat while I was asleep. The house was dead quiet except for the swishing of the ceiling fan. Around and around it went. I finally had a day off. I had been picking up a ton of hours at work since me and Lox broke up, just working to keep my mind off of how hurt I was feeling. Yes, we broke up. Once I saw those videos of him and Sahnai, I decided he was like all other men—a liar, cheater, and not worth my time. It had not been easy, but I decided to get up and brush myself off, stand on my tens with no man, and just enjoy life. I guessed me lying on the couch listening to the fan was enjoying life.

Lox had been trying everything to get me back, and I mean everything: sending me dozens of roses, Edible Arrangements, and even my favorite candies. Last week, I came home to a guy on my doorstep holding a bear as big as him and a bunch of balloons. The day after, it was purses—several purses all wrapped up from Saks Fifth Avenue. It had Azia written all over it. We all knew she was the queen of shopping. Then came the kids. He tried to use the kids to lure me back in. I still got li'l Q and Aiden a lot, Aiden less than Q because his illness kept him in the hospital or home sick most of the time.

Vivy was with Lox more than me some weeks, and even though I told myself it was because she wanted to hang out with Kadia when she was over, I knew it was because she loved him. I would admit some days I was tempted to run back into his arms, fuck the shit out of him, then tell him how much I loved him and how miserable I was without him, but I had been holding strong.

Bam! Bam! Bam! Someone banged on my door so loud I fell off the couch. I could feel my heart racing as I ran to the door and pulled back the curtain a little, only to see the UPS man calmly walking away like he didn't just almost give me a fucking heart attack. Looking down, all I saw were brown boxes piled in front of the door. More gifts. I wished Lennox would leave well enough alone. What happened with him and his baby mom happened, and we needed to move forward. We were still friends for the kids' sake, so there was no reason for all this.

Seeing him walk back from the truck with two more packages, I snatched the door open so hard I hurt my arm a little. I politely held out my hand for the rest of the boxes.

"Ma'am, please sign right here," the UPS guy said while looking me up and down with his creepy little eyes. Snatching the clipboard, I rolled my eyes and tugged on my little mint green shorts, like that was going to cover me more. Not saying another word to the creep, I slammed the door in his face and flung myself back on the couch, throwing the boxes next to me.

Picking up the phone, I dialed Azia, hoping she picked up. "Hey, boo, what are you up to?" her cheerful voice filled the line.

"Azia, stop playing with me. You know why I am calling. I am opening more boxes from Nordstrom filled with more expensive purses, shoes, and what is this, a Gucci belt?" I yelled in the direction of the phone that I had placed on speaker so my hands were free. "Azia, don't be quiet now. I know it is you picking out all this shit for your cousin to send to me. I also know you are taking his money and buying a bunch of the same for yourself. Stop buying shit. I am running out of space. I don't want to encourage Lox, and the UPS guy is starting to freak me the hell out."

Laughter was the only response I heard from the other end of the phone. "Hey, if my cousin wants to fund shopping sprees for both of us, who am I to argue or disagree? You need to pick some shit out that you want. Ooh, we should do furniture next. Make him redo the whole house. Hell, let's buy a new house."

Shit, Azia really had a shopping problem. I needed her to get a new man or just some dick. This was getting out of hand. Before you knew it, I would have a houseful of furniture, purses, and shoes. I was about to start selling this shit on eBay or something and adding the proceeds to Vivy's college fund. "Azia, you are not listening. No more gifts. If I am going to ever forgive Lox, not saying I am, especially after the club shit the other day, gifts are not going to be the reason why. Now I'ma get off this phone and go Google you a shopper's anonymous meeting."

"You know, Alani, I wish Inaya would hurry and drop that baby . . . I mean, my niece or nephew who I will love so much, so we can have a girls' weekend. We could go to Toronto and hit the strip clubs and get lit. Oh, yeah, and maybe stop at just one mall. We can take Phantom's credit card if it makes you feel better. I'ma respect your wishes, and no more gifts, for now. We have a baby to shop for and a baby shower to plan, so I can focus my spending addiction in that direction," Azia said with so much happiness and joy in her voice.

"Well, Azia, you did hit on something. We have to think about the baby shower. If it's a boy—I hope not a boy because a little Phantom will just be unkind to humanity—but if it is a boy, we can do like a royal theme with blue and gold. I saw these adorable candy apples with those colors on Pinterest the other day. We can have a candy table with huge lollipops and blue rock candies and M&Ms. I can't wait. I think we should book the venue today. We can pick a date for January so she won't be that pregnant when the time comes and she can enjoy it," I gushed, finally feeling excited about something. Since seeing Lox with that ratchet bitch in the club the other night, I had been feeling low. I just didn't want to admit it to anyone. This baby shower may be the distraction I needed.

After going over more baby shower options, me and Azia decided to book Mario's, an Italian restaurant, for the baby shower on January 22. I decided to go pay Inaya a visit after I took a nap. I really deserved this nap. I kept dreaming about Lox—the way he talked, touched me, and fucked me. I had not had any rest in a while, but I was in need today. Making my way upstairs, I grabbed my iPad and googled Pornhub. Typing in my password, I went right for my saved premium videos. Taking my silver bullet out, I watched as this big-dick-ass nigga began laying the pipe on some little, skinny young girl. Just looking at his dick turned me on. That was how horny I was. Seeing him nut all over her face brought me to my orgasm, and I was finally able to roll over and get some sleep.

When I woke up the next day, I realized I had not set the alarm, so I overslept. Jumping out of bed, I grabbed my cell in one hand as I ran to the bathroom, tripping over my robe that I dropped on the floor. I was clean, but I was not neat. Inaya was always over here picking shit up. Once I made it to the master bathroom, I texted my manager, Marsha, with one hand, telling her I was on the way, and brushed my teeth with the other. I was happy my mom had Vivy today because I would have really been pushing Marsha's buttons had I missed the manager's meeting. Snatching the first business dress I could see, a cute gray Calvin Klein dress that flared at the bottom and cut a little in the breast area, I threw some coconut oil on my hair and pulled it back in a bun. Running downstairs, I grabbed some ankle boots and almost broke my ankle trying to get in them as I ran out the door.

As soon as I got to the car, I realized I had no idea where my keys were. *Fuck, I had to use them to lock the front door, so where could they be?* Searching my Gucci tote bag and my cream leather briefcase, I came up with nothing. *Well, damn, I get some rest and my morning is all over the place.* Walking back to the door to see if they fell on the ground, there were my keys, still hanging from the doorknob. Snatching them and doing a quick 180, I jumped in my car and peeled out of the driveway. I swore today it seemed like every dumb driver in the state of New York was on the road either cutting me off only to drive slow in front of me or just being in the fucking way. Finally, I pulled up to the cute little office building located in the Twelve Corners Plaza.

As soon as I walked in, I rushed to put my stuff away and grab a coffee. Looking at the time, I realized I needed to throw on some lip gloss to make this manager's meeting at ten a.m. Walking in, I was happy I made it on time because I could see Marsha was on one today. She was standing at the front of the room with her dry-erase marker in one hand and a pointer in the other. "Good morning, everyone. Today we have some big news to discuss." She began making lists on the white board and jotting down names under the main categories. "Alani will be taking the lead on the decorating and landscape design on this property. I expect everyone to do whatever task it is she gives you as soon as she gives them to you," Marsha said, breaking me out of my trance.

Turning to me, she continued, "Alani, we need this project completed by the tenth of November, and we cannot have any delays. Also, the decor must be impeccable. The company needs this sale. Please remember that the commissions from sales are how you are paid. I expect a completed project plan by the end of the day." With that, my boss, Marsha, walked away from me, flipping her hair. I never knew with her if she liked me or hated me. I guessed she must have at least respected me to give me this project, unless she just wanted me to fail.

Seeing my three coworkers snickering behind their hands and whispering, I knew they were talking about me. See, the old ignorant me would have gone and grabbed the nearest object and beat their asses, but for what? Yes, I was frustrated because it sucked when your team was looking at you like they had no confidence in you. The worst part was that these people sat in my face every day, laughed and joked with me, hell, some even said they were my friend. These were the motherfuckers who were waiting to see me fail. *It's cool, though. I bet I won't be failing. Fuck them.*

Grabbing a fresh orange from the cafeteria, I made my way back to my desk. Leaning back in my chair, I looked down at my manicured nails. Instead of picturing the deep purple nails roaming over Lox's chest, I was thinking about my hand intertwined with his. I missed Lox, not just the sex, but the comfort I received from him. I loved the way he was not scared to be silly no matter where we were. He was not one of those over-macho type niggas, like Phantom. But for real, he didn't have a problem holding my hand anywhere or letting me jump on his back. He was a go-with-the-flow kinda guy.

Picking up the phone, I shot him a text before I could talk sense into myself.

Me: You good?

Heartbreaker: Yeah, what's up? Everything good with you and baby girl?

Me: Vivy misses you guys. I am okay. Have a big project at work, and I am kinda nervous about it.

Heartbreaker: Oh, yeah? What kind of project got my baby nervous? You know whatever it is, you got this, ma, trust.

Me: Marsha gave me the chance to decorate a historical house in the South Wedge. You know those houses are virtually mansions. I have to do the design for the landscaping as well. It has to be big because the company could make millions on this sale. So I am sitting here trying to come up with a theme and figure out what should go where.

Heartbreaker: Ma, go get it, this project is yours. This is your thang and I believe in you. Why don't you make a video using iVideo for the presentation?

Me: Good idea. I'ma do that instead of a standard PowerPoint presentation. Thank you. You always know the right things to say to make shit right. I still ain't fucking with you, though.

Heartbreaker: Damn, ma, for real, it's like that? I'm not stopping until I have you back in my life, so I am not giving up. And I meant what I said about taking you out to celebrate. If you want, it can be a family dinner so you will have your girls there to keep you safe. LOL.

Me: Okay, bye, Lox. Have a good day.

Resting my head in my hands for a moment, I felt tingling run through my body. I still got excited at the thought of Lox. I was still not giving in to him. I did that with my daughter's father, only to have him murdered for cheating on me, then being stuck with Pandora's box with the lid blown off after. The secrets were enough to keep me up at night still if I thought about them too much. It wasn't just the cheating or the kids that hurt me. It was the extent of the relationships he was having while with me. These were some real Jay and Bey type shit, not a hit it and quit it. He had family pictures with these bitches, Valentine's Day vacation, and Christmas dinners. All those times I was home alone with our baby and he was working, it was all a lie. I wondered when he even found time to peddle those guns between fucking and licking and making babies.

Loading up my computer, I grabbed my wireless mouse, threw on my headphones so I could get lost in my work, and began clicking on several images of couches, tables, wall art, and a garden plan. I then incorporated everything into a video trailer with an appropriate matching song. Bringing my USB into Marsha's office, I knocked lightly on the door.

"Hello, Marsha. I have put together a video trailer for a proposal. I also attached slides, so if the client would like something changed, we could update the model. Please let me know what you think." I waited for her to say something. Instead, she nodded her head and gave me a big smile before turning in her chair and going back to work. *Well, looks like I made it through another day of work.* I was ready to go home, have some wine, and go to sleep, but I had to pick up Vivian and deal with my mother, whom I loved dearly, some days.

As soon as I pulled up, I could see my mom looking through the window, peeking through her curtains like a criminal. Walking in, I called out to Vivy to come on and tried to make it back to the door quickly. No such luck. "Mommy, I wanted Lox to come with you to pick me up," Vivy whined. Seeing that my mom was suddenly in front of me, I was not able to run in and run out without hearing a lecture from her.

"So, Alani Janae, you mean to tell me you have not forgiven Lennox as of yet? Little girl, do you want to be alone all of your life? I understand you were hurt, but he is different. Hell, even if he is not, you need someone in your life. This being alone and pitiful shit is not cute," she lectured as I tried to ease closer to the door without disrespecting my mother.

"Mom, what about me demanding respect for myself? I am not teaching Vivy that women should accept any treatment just so they are not alone. I am sorry if you're hurt, but that thinking is retarded and backward. That is the problem with young black women. They stand for nothing and fall for anything, but not this black woman. I ain't falling for shit. Now if you will excuse me, good night." Walking out the door with Vivy in hand, I didn't even look back. I had had enough for one day.

Pulling up to my house to find a black-on-black Range Rover in my parking lot, I knew it was Lox. Now I was going to struggle with my emotions all over again.

Seeing him jump out of the truck, Vivy ran and jumped in his arms. Watching him twirl her around in a circle and seeing her squeal in delight almost had me jealous. I wanted him to swing me in a circle and laugh with me, smile at me. Urghh. That was when I noticed Azia hopping out on the other side.

"Bihh, get ready, we gonna go out tonight. You look like you need a drink or several drinks. Shit, Vivy going with her stepdaddy for the weekend, so she's good. Now, come on, let's go," demanded Azia while pulling me in the house to get ready.

Lox

Wow, Alani was looking good. Even in her work clothes, her fat ass was sticking out and making my dick hard. Looking back at a smiling Vivy, I decided to stop and get pizza for her and Kadia. Since Phantom had been back, Kadia had not been back to her house. She was a stubborn little girl and had Phantom wrapped around her pinky finger. Hell, she had all of us wrapped around her finger. I guessed she got that stubborn shit from her mama. Speaking of moms, when I pulled up to my house, I could see my mom's Nissan Versa sitting in my driveway. I didn't know why she got that weird-ass car. I tried to buy her a Lexus or at least a Camry, but no, she saw it in a commercial and fell in love.

"Hello," I called as I opened the door with food in one hand and Vivy's bag in the other.

"Vivy, I am so glad you came to stay with me. I missed you so much. Let's go play with my new toy my daddy bought me today!" yelled an excited Kadia, who wouldn't stop hopping around and hugging Vivy, even though they saw each other in school today. Laughing as they ran off, my face turned into a frown when I noticed the extra people in my house.

"Yo, nigga, who the fuck are you? And, Dana, I told you I wasn't fucking with you no more, so move your ass up outta my crib. Both of y'all, move along now." I could feel my skin turning red, and my hand was itching to shoot someone. I was pretty much done with all of my family. I just didn't have the heart to turn my back on my mom, even though she was just another weak woman who clearly didn't respect herself.

"Lennox, why would you speak to your sister that way? I know I raised you both better than that. I know she messed up, but she needs your help, and she needs you to be there for her," she cried as she pleaded Dana's case.

The thing was, I was not really mad that Dana was trying to defend me. I was just mad at how she did it. Sahnai was not always innocent in what she did, but she wasn't going to be fucking my pops, and I knew that li'l Q was all me. I was just angry because she could have injured one of my sons while she was there trying to slice and dice their mama. Inspecting the boy they brought along with them, I realized he must be Dana's friend because he was standing close to her and rubbing her arm. He was shaking while doing it, though, little bitch ass. I was surprised to see my sister with a man. Honestly, my pops wasn't the only one who thought she was going to end up licking clits instead of taking dicks. She had always been weird as hell. Maybe that was why we were not close. If I didn't know any better, I would have sworn she had different parents.

"Ma, you don't have to defend me. Lox is a pussy, and I should have stabbed him instead. That is what I get for caring about someone who ain't shit." Before my sister could even finish her sentence good, I had my hands around her neck. I instantly loosened my grip because I was not into hurting females. I just lost my temper thinking of all the things I had done for my sister. *What an ungrateful little bitch.* When she was ten and set her hair on fire to see what would happen, I saved her. When she was twelve and got chased home by a bunch of kids who said she was watching them undress in the locker room, I saved her. I paid for all the fun shit she wanted—clothes, music, and even vacations because my dad didn't think it was important. Only school was important in his eyes. *None of these hoes are loyal, I see.* Feeling some soft shit touch my arm, I realized her little punk-ass boyfriend was trying to hit me or rub me or some shit. I snatched her up in one hand and him in the other and threw them out my front door before I ended up doing something I regretted with my kids upstairs.

Watching my mother as she slowly followed the two unwanted guests to the car with her head down and back bent, I realized I didn't feel bad. She should have done something about that child a long time ago, and now it was too late. Hell, Azia was more of a sister to me than she was. Azia and Inaya helped with the kids, the house, and were down when it came time to help me win back Alani. They even interviewed the nannies for me so I could pick a good one since I couldn't be over here with the babies alone all the time. Thinking about my no-good baby mamas pissed me off all over again. Sending Sahnai's phone a text, I let her know I was done playing with her.

Me: When I find you, trust me, it will not be good. What kind of mother abandons her son and never looks back? I hope you know there is no showing your face around here again.

Seeing I had a few unanswered messages, I scrolled through them. A few bitches I fucked from time to time were sending me ass shots and invites to come over. One of the girls was the clown-ass bitch from the club the other night. She was friends with Phantom's people, so I tried not to hurt her feelings and shit, but I made it clear from the jump I had a woman and we were just taking a break. Seeing one from Alani made me smile even though it wasn't about me.

My Love: Hey, just making sure the kids are okay. Tell them I love them, and give the kids a kiss for me. Give Aiden two.

Me: No kiss for me?

Laughing because she sent me the middle finger emoji, I decided not to push my luck and leave my boo alone. I was happy she was at least talking to me, and no matter how mad she was, she always checked on the kids. That was why I always checked for her. She was better than their no-good-ass mamas. I couldn't believe I let some pussy get in the way of the special thing we had going. I just hoped I got one more chance to be with her.

Inaya

Today was the day me and Phantom went to find out the sex of the baby. Lately, he had been avoiding me even when staying in the same house. He came in and slept in Kadia's room, closing the door behind him. He had been quiet, not talking shit or trying to feel me up. I guessed he got serious with his new bitch and I had just become a duty to him. I had been tense the past few weeks. I hadn't told anyone, but I was desperately hoping for a boy. There were already a lot of boys between Azia's kids and Lox's sons, but if this baby was a girl, it would be Phantom's real daughter, and I didn't know where that would leave Kadia. He loved her for now, but if his real daughter came along, that may change things. Especially because of the way he felt about me. He hadn't put me down in a long time, but there were moments I could see it in his eyes. And thinking about how he loved me one moment and hated me the next made me afraid to my core that he would hate my daughter that way once he had his own.

Shaking off the bad vibes, I began the slow process of getting dressed. I was only five months, but it felt like I was a year. I prayed there was only one baby in there, because I could barely manage Kadia, and the thought of two more small people made my head spin and palms sweat. I had no idea how Azia managed it all. She had a lot of patience. Shit, she had to deal with Phantom's and Lox's asses along with her three children. *Lox got her out here living like a personal shopper or relationship counselor trying to fix his mess with Alani and Phantom.*

Well, he was just him, miserable as hell, and I noticed lately he had been drinking like a fish.

Slipping my feet into my purple Ugg slippers, I stood up and yanked my black tights over my belly for the second time. Every time I sat down, the tights would roll off the top of my round belly. Last thing to go on was my black and purple striped sweater with the turtleneck. I was sweating, but I knew as soon as I got outside in the fall air, I would be cold as hell. Fall air in Upstate NY was like winter air in other places.

"Yo, ma, we gonna be late. You a'ight in there?" Phantom's sexy voice asked from the other side of my bedroom door.

Not bothering to respond since I was still trying to catch my breath, I opened the bedroom door so he could see I at least had clothes on. Brushing my long hair back into a bun, I was out of breath and struggling before I even got any damn where. *Four more months of this shit, and I ain't even that big yet. Great, I have a lot to look forward to.* Swirling the makeup brush in my summer peach blush from MAC, I dabbed it on my cheeks in a fast, twirling motion, threw on some plum lip gloss, and smacked my lips while looking in the dresser mirror. I guessed sexy was out of the question with my belly sticking out, but I did try to look nice in front of Phantom. Even though my mind told me fuck him, my heart still longed for his love.

Feeling his hand pop my behind, my pregnant pussy began working overtime, producing juices that should not have been that hot or wet. Rolling my eyes, but smiling on the inside, I was enjoying his touch. Waddling my way downstairs, I was happy that Phantom headed toward his Bentley. I was always tired with this pregnancy, and I hated driving these days. I was surprised he would even bring that car over in this area, but I forgot how cocky his ass was. As soon as I was seated in the soft leather seats, I could feel my eyes closing and my body relaxing. It was like a slice of heaven when the heat in the heated seats kicked in. Hearing Phantom on his phone, I didn't even open one eye to pay attention to who he was talking to.

"Inaya, did you hear what I said to you?" he said while lightly touching my arm.

"Huh? I was half-asleep and not paying attention," I replied while yawning and sitting up a little.

"That was Azia, and she said why the hell have you been ignoring her texts all morning? You have to check her texts now. You not mad at my little sis, are you? I know she said she was not going to tell you what to do as far as living here and not somewhere safe or any of the other shit you being hardheaded about. Hell, I can barely get Azia's ass to speak to me because of you, so you shouldn't be mad at her."

Shaking my head and laughing, I had to tell him why I was ignoring my sister. Yeah, she was my sister too. I loved her ass so much. She was always there in my corner, not judging me, lecturing me, or telling me to give Phantom another chance. Shit, I hadn't heard from my own cousin in months. After lots of calls and messages, I came to the conclusion she just didn't give a fuck about me or anyone else for that matter.

"Phantom, I am ignoring Azia's ass this morning be- cause all she wants to talk about is the gender of the baby and how she wants to know first thing so we can go shopping and basically spend all of your money. I am too broke and too tired to go shopping. No one likes shopping as much as she does. But just to satisfy her since she called my prison warden to check on me, I am going to respond to her texts."

He laughed and shook his head. "Yeah, my sister is a damn beast in the mall. Maybe I should just make an investment and buy her ass a mall or shopping center. Maybe she will get tired of shopping then."

I looked at him, and our eyes met at the same time. We both said, "Nah."

Looking at my phone, I saw I had two missed calls and ten texts from Azia. The first ones were just what I thought: Good morning, can't wait to shop for the baby, so hurry to your appointment, and a few images of baby shit I could never afford. Bad enough they had Kadia walking around here dressed like she was North West or some other celebrity child. Then there was a video labeled Alani after a drunken night. Pressing play, I laughed so hard I almost peed myself. Calling Azia right away, I could hear her choking on laughter as she answered.

"Hello? I knew your punk ass was going to be calling once you saw the damn video. I took Miss Alani out last night since she told me I should stop using Lox's money to buy her stuff—well, buy me stuff too—so I figured some liquor would loosen her up and help her think about some stuff she would like to buy on his black card. I have been trying to get some new furniture for both of us. I didn't know she was a soft drinker. Okay, well, maybe I was giving her double shots in her drink unbeknownst to her, but still, a soft drinker."

Trying to keep my face straight since Phantom was looking at me like I had lost my mind, I continued our conversation. "Azia, when I saw her wake up with one shoe on, a Snickers bar partially eaten in her hand and her clothes half on, I didn't know whether to laugh or cry. Oh, and her hair looked like she stuck her finger in a light socket while it was soaking wet and lightning outside. Why, just tell me why she had one arm in her shirt and her pants were at her ankles. Did she sleep like that?" I was laughing so hard I had tears rolling down my cheeks.

Realizing we were pulling into the hospital parking lot, I ended my call with Azia telling me to hurry and find out because she had Saks Fifth Avenue pulled up on her tablet. Opening my own side of the car and preparing to get out, I noticed that Phantom was jogging around to me. Holding out his hand, he pulled me up and closed the door behind me. He smelled good, like always. I think he had on Armani Code today. That cologne went well with his natural scent. He was looking like a snack in some blue jeans and a black Armani hoodie with black leather Clarks. As soon as we walked in, women were openly flirting with him. *Like damn, all these hoes see is some bling and fresh clothes, and they are throwing pussy. This is a fucking ultrasound office, which means some, if not all, of these thotsicles must be pregnant, yet they're still breaking their necks to look at my baby daddy, licking their lips and trying to slide him phone numbers.*

I decided to be petty and snuggle up as close as I could get on the little waiting room chairs. Laying my head on his shoulder, I played in his braids and kissed on his neck. He didn't push me away, and I thanked God for that because if he played me in front of these bitches, I would have punched him in his throat. Being pregnant made me a little more vicious than I used to be. Hearing him blow out his breath, I realized I was turning him on. *Good shit, I really need some dick sometime soon and it ain't like I can fuck anybody else. He better get on board, or I am going to let Marvin eat the pussy or something. I have never been this horny in my life.*

"Inaya Walker," the nurse called. We both stood up, and I grabbed his hand as we walked past the thot gallery.

Making sure they could hear me, I called out to the nurse, "Hello, this is my husband, Jahdair, and I am Inaya. It is such a shame more fathers are not here to

see their baby's first picture. I guess I got a good one."
Looking back, I could see the haters rolling their eyes and
kissing their teeth. *Oh, well, don't come for me or mine
next time. Ol' lonely-ass bitches who don't know who
their baby daddies are.*

As soon as we were in the room and the tech was
talking to us, I was starting to panic again. Pulling up
my sweater and pulling down my tights, I could hear
Phantom suck in his breath in shock, and he ran his hand
along the light red line the tights left on my belly.

"Inaya, what the fuck, man? You always doing some
shit. Don't be suffocating my baby in these tight-ass
pants. You going to the store for some clothes that fit,
and I don't want to hear shit about it. If you don't take
the money and go buy them, I am sending Azia's ass, and
she's gonna bring back the whole store," he chastised
and threatened me at the same time.

"Sir, it is really not that tight, and the baby is fine. The
line could just be from her sitting in the car," offered the
technician.

Not responding to either one of them, I closed my
eyes and began to pray to God for a boy. I tensed as
soon as I felt the cold gel touch my belly. Hearing the
heartbeat, I felt Phantom squeeze my hand tight, and
I could tell he was feeling emotional, even though he
would never admit it. "Here is the head and the hand,
and over here is the baby's spine," the lady said, pointing at the big screen before us. She began taking pictures
and writing little notes like "Hi, Mom!" and "Hi, Dad!"
on them. "Do you want to know the sex of the baby?"
Shaking my head slightly, letting her know that I did, I
held my breath. "Okay, let's see if this baby will cooperate
and let us see. Yes, there we go, you are having a little girl.
Congratulations, you two," she said, wiping off my belly
and telling me she would go get our pictures. Before she

could even leave the room, I began to cry. My worst fear had come true. Kadia would be shoved aside for this baby. She would have no father again, and it was my fault. If I hadn't gotten pregnant, then she would still have had a father in Phantom. Now, he would only have love for his daughter.

Both the tech and Phantom were watching me like I had lost my mind, and with the way I was crying, I felt like I might have. I was sobbing so hard I couldn't breathe, and my body was shaking. I knew my makeup was all over my face and snot was probably dripping. I felt Phantom put his hand on my back to calm me down, but it didn't work. Before I could stop it, I was leaning over and throwing up all over the floor of the room. I began choking a little until I sat all the way up.

"Ma'am, are you okay? I am going to get a nurse in here, but you have to calm down. Your file said you just got your pregnancy under control, and we do not want to send your blood pressure back up again," the tech said to me in a panicked voice. As she ran out of the room, Phantom climbed on the bed and pulled me into his lap, rocking me in his arms. I closed my eyes and tried to imagine that this was a boy, that they made a mistake so I could get myself calm. I didn't want to harm our baby. I swear I didn't.

"Iny, what is wrong, ma? I am right here, the baby is okay, and Kades is fine. You have to relax. I am not going away again. I am going to be here when the baby comes, I promise," he said in a reassuring tone.

"Jahdair, you don't understand. I didn't want a girl, and I needed this baby to be a boy. I don't want you to throw Kadia to the side because you will be having a real daughter now. If I didn't get pregnant, she wouldn't be without a father again. This is my fault. I can never do good enough for her. I should just give her up for adoption, but I don't even know who to give her to," I cried, trying not to look at his face. I didn't want to see the truth in what I was saying.

"Inaya, this pregnancy has messed with your brain. Are you losing it? Hell, I bet it is because those pants are too fucking tight, and they are cutting off the oxygen to your brain. Kades is my real daughter. The minute I told her she could call me her daddy, I meant it. She will never have another father. Even if we have five more girls, she will always have space in my heart as my daughter. Hell, even if you think you gonna settle down with Marvin the Clown, I am still her only daddy. I don't know what kind of bum-ass niggas you were messing with, but I do know I am not one of 'em. Shit, I've wanted to tell you I want us to change Kadia's last name to Lucas for a while now. I just didn't want you to piss me off with no nonsense, so I was waiting to say anything. But we need to do that soon. Shit, we can go to the county clerk's office tomorrow and handle that. She should have my last name, and I should be listed on her birth certificate. You have nothing to worry about, so get yourself together so you and Azia can go buy both of my daughters some shit."

I gave him a weak smile, and he leaned down and kissed my forehead. The doctor and nurse burst through the door, ruining our intimate moment by poking all over me and putting that damn blood pressure cuff around my arm so it could squeeze the shit out of me. "Now, Inaya, you do not want to be back here on bed rest. Your blood pressure is slightly elevated, but your legs are not swollen, so instead of admitting you, I am telling you I need you to relax. No more stress or nonsense. I see you have someone by your side, and I know your two sisters would do anything for you because they didn't leave your side when you were admitted last time. Why don't you let them help you? Don't be stubborn. This is your life and the baby's life we are talking about."

Nodding my head in agreement, I slowly got off the side of the bed and made my way to the restroom to rinse my mouth out.

Taking the papers the receptionist handed me as we checked out, I felt physically exhausted. I wanted to go buy something for our new baby, but honestly, I didn't want to bring anything back to the house I was living in now. Shit, I didn't know how I was going to work this out, because we only had two bedrooms, and Kadia's room was small. I hated to ask Phantom for anything or give in to his demands of moving, so for now, I was just going to start looking at what else I could afford on my own. I didn't want him to think I was using him or that he won and now had control over me.

The next few weeks really flew by as I became so busy with end-of-semester schoolwork and all of the new clients my company was preparing for. I guessed in the New Year people wanted to find ways to invest their money, so they called, ready to hand over cash. I was excited to see we got a Christmas bonus of $3,000. Even though it was only November, it was truly coming at the perfect time. I could go out on Black Friday, according to Azia, who said this was her favorite holiday, and shop, and I could save some for a deposit on a new place. I wanted to be moved before my newest angel made her appearance.

Thanksgiving was only a few days away, and I was trying my hardest to stay in the holiday spirit. One good thing was that I was off of work and school for one full week, and I would be going to stay with Azia. I missed the family and Kadia. She still wouldn't come back to the house, saying she hated it here and she was scared. Packing the last of my stuff, I walked to the Audi, throwing my two bags in the back so I could make my way out to the Reserve where Lox and Azia lived. As soon as I pulled into the driveway, I saw Alani's little blue car parked. It was going to be nice to have her here, even though I knew she was avoiding Lox. I noticed that my little cousin Nadia was here, too, and sitting on the couch when I walked in.

"Inaya, I missed you so much. Lox came and got me so I could spend the holidays with you guys," she explained in an excited tone as I walked over and gave her a hug.

"What about Grams? I don't want her to be alone," I said.

"Grams and her two friends are on a cruise in the Bahamas. She said this is the perfect time, right at the end of hurricane season, and she knew I would be here with you guys, so she is enjoying a little free time, as she called it. She said she loves you, though." Hell, I wasn't mad at all. My grandmother spent her whole life raising everyone else's kids, even after hers were grown, because no one's parents wanted to step up and do their jobs. "I can't wait to go Black Friday shopping with you and the girls. Me and Azia already made a list and a plan so we can hit all the good stores and get the best deals. Then on Monday we get to do it online, too. And guess what, Iny. Lox and Phantom gave me money to shop with since I am getting all A's in school, and Grams told them how good I was being around the house. Isn't that nice?" Nadia said with more excitement than I had ever heard in her voice.

"Oh, boy, Azia, I think you have finally found your shopping partner. You all are creating another monster and don't even see it." I wasn't really mad about it. I wanted to be a better big cousin than Sahnai was to me, so I felt it was important for Nadia to be well taken care of. If I could have somehow found a bigger place, I would have taken her to come live with me. Our grandmother was getting up there in years and was getting tired. Plus,

Nadia needed someone young to keep an eye on her, because I remembered how easy it was to fall into trouble at that age. Especially trouble concerning boys.

Hurrying to the couch so I could relax and watch my show, *Modern Family,* I took out the *Apartment Finder* magazine so I could look through it while waiting for it to come on. I loved watching comedies on TV, and this one always made me laugh. Feeling someone watching me, I looked up to see Lox's mom. "Good evening, Auntie Sena. How have you been?" I asked her. She seemed hesitant to come and sit with me. *I think she is still embarrassed by all that happened with her husband and Toya. Shit, it was not her fault. You cannot control other people one bit and cannot beat yourself up trying.*

Slowly, she came and sat next to me. We spent the next hour talking and catching up. She told me how happy she was to have another little girl to spoil besides Vivy and Kadia. I agreed that having another girl would be nice. Hell, what was I thinking wanting another Phantom to deal with?

"Inaya, I see you're looking for apartments. Have you found anything else in a better area? I know it is not really my business, but Phantom is like my son, so this baby is like my grandbaby. You know I love you like a daughter-in-law. I know what it is like to be heartbroken. I promise, I do. You cannot allow emotions to control you to the point where you are not taking the best care of you and your children. These children, Kadia, and the new baby are Phantom's responsibility. I did not raise him to back away from his responsibility, and more than that, he loves you guys. Allow him to be a man and do what he should be doing to care for you and the children," she pleaded with sad eyes.

I didn't know how to be hardheaded and stubborn and tell her I was okay with the situation I was in now.

How do you say that to someone who is truly concerned about you and who is pouring out her heart to you? Especially when it is all a lie. I was not all right. I had just found out my job didn't provide paid maternity leave, so I would have to find a way to go back to work immediately after having the baby. I had no idea what I was going to do about daycare or any of it. I was truly just tired of struggling and busting my ass at work and school. "I understand he is trying to be nice and he feels sorry for me, but he left me. I cannot accept anything from him." I offered my weak explanation as best I could in hopes that she would drop the subject. I knew Phantom should be taking care of us and it was his job, but I didn't want anyone who didn't love me to do shit for me.

"Inaya, come and take a walk with me. Please, I know you are being respectful and not cursing at me or telling me to mind my own business, even though maybe you want to. I need to show you something and it is important."

Getting up slowly, I slid my feet into my slippers and grabbed my gray peacoat from the hook. Noticing Lox's mom grab a set of keys from her handbag, I assumed they were to Azia's place or maybe even Lox's.

Walking out into the cool night air, I hoped we would not be out here long. I was freezing. Following close behind Aunt Sena as we walked past Lox's house on the left and up a long driveway to the house next door, curiosity was beginning to get the best of me. The front of the house was amazing. It had a light brown brick exterior with huge windows, and the garden out front was filled with colorful flowers. This was the kind of house I always wanted to live in. *I wonder if this is her house. It would make sense if it is.* Maybe she just wanted to speak to me in a more private setting.

"Inaya, once when Lennox was small and his sister wasn't even born yet, I found out his father was cheating on me. Only this time was not like the others. He wasn't just having sex with this girl or messing around with her. They were in a real relationship. He had clothes in her house and had even bought her a ring as a sign of him wanting to marry her someday. I was crushed. Lennox told me he was leaving but would take care of me and the baby because that was his job.

"Instead of accepting his help, I grabbed Lox and left in a fit of anger and sadness. I left the city and went back to the country where I was from and moved in with my mother. Now let me explain something. There were already two of my sisters and their children living in this small house that my mother owned. There was barely food, and we all had to find a way to pitch in. One day after a few months of me not working because I could not find a job, my mother threw me out with my baby. She couldn't afford for us to be there anymore. Lox became very ill as we lived from place to place, sleeping outside sometimes. I almost lost my son because I let a broken heart stop me from accepting the help I deserved and needed, that my son deserved and needed. What if Kadia had been home with you when you were robbed? What if it happens again once you have the baby? I know you are a smart girl."

Thinking about her story made my head and my heart ache, and I could imagine her young and scared, all alone, taking care of her son. I felt tears fall as we walked into her house. "Auntie, I am sorry you went through all of that. I am glad it worked out and that Lox was saved. He is a good egg. Also, your house is amazing. I love it here. Are you asking me to live with you?" I asked in a confused voice.

"Child, this is not my house. I live in a different area altogether. I am too old to be keeping up with a place this big. This is your house, the house that Phantom had built for you. It's empty for now because he wanted you to pick out your own stuff, but it was created for you because of the love he has for you but doesn't know how to express."

"My house?" I asked with a stutter. She nodded her head and stood near the door as I walked through the house. The kitchen was perfect. It had the pretty backsplash in gray and white, and in the middle of the room stood the island I always wanted. When me and Phantom were together, we always watched HGTV. Well, I watched and he talked shit, but I guessed he was listening to all the things I loved in a house, because they were all here. Seeing all the space in the downstairs area, I was impressed. Taking the stairs, I wondered what I would find once I got to the bedrooms.

The first two bedrooms I opened were huge but empty inside. Stopping in front of a door with a gold crown and Kadia's name below, I was excited to see my little girl's room. Opening the door, I couldn't help but take a deep breath. It was like something out of a magazine. The walls were white, except her accent wall, which was painted half pink and half purple, with gold pictures and accessories all over the room. The bed looked like a queen size and had a pink fabric headboard with what looked like gold stripes in a diamond pattern. The blanket was the same purple from the wall, with pink and gold hearts and crowns printed on it. There were matching pillows and gold fur throw rugs. She even had two custom-made chairs, one gold and one pink, in the shape of princess crowns.

Kadia is going to love this room. I didn't see any toys except a dollhouse, so I assumed that the toys would be going to the playroom. *Good, a room I can close the door on and not have to clean day in and day out.* Making my way to the master bedroom, I cracked the door and opened it, expecting to see another empty room. Instead, I saw a king-sized bed with all white sheets and nothing else on it. The bedroom set was cute and looked like furniture I would pick out. The wood was a light cream color with darker accents around the swirls that were carved into a cute pattern. The dressers and end tables matched. The room was a mess with clothes all over the floor and one picture on the table next to the unmade bed. Sinking down on the fluffy mattress, I could smell Phantom's scent, and it made me smile. Picking up the cheap dollar store frame, I noticed a picture of me and Kadia in front of her school. We were both grinning, and she had her arms around my waist.

Damn, its shit like this that fucks my head up. Does he really love me like I want to believe he does? Should I just move into this house? It seems like it was made for me and our kids. Closing my eyes, I decided to pray and ask God what to do. "God, I don't know what to do. This house is amazing, and it feels so right here, but Phantom has hurt me so badly. I want to do the right thing. God, please give me a sign. Amen." Getting up and wandering over to the closet, I opened the door, only to find it led to a smaller bedroom. This one was empty as well, except I could see some stuff piled up in the closet. Walking into the closet, I sat down and started looking through the bags of stuff. There were tons of baby shoes, mostly Jordans, and tiny matching newborn hats. There were a few little onesies that read "I Love Daddy," matching bibs, and at the bottom of the last bag, there was a baby book. Opening the book, I could tell Phantom was the one who bought it because the places written on were in his handwriting.

This was the sign from God. *I am not going to keep fighting this man who obviously loves his children even if he doesn't love me. I am going to move in the house and make the best of it. I will even consider taking money from him. I will have to survive somehow after I have the baby, and I do not want my newborn baby with strangers. I am sure we can sit down and come up with a reasonable amount of money—not thousands a month.*

Walking back downstairs to meet Phantom's aunt, I found her staring out of the bay windows in the living room. "Auntie, I am going to stay here tonight if you don't mind. Can you just tell Phantom I am going to move into the house? Your job is done. I am not mad at you at all. I thank you for helping me see what I was missing all along." I gave her a hug as she smiled and walked back to Azia's house.

I realized I had no clothes here or anything, but it didn't matter. I went upstairs and stripped down to my panties and grabbed one of Phantom's T-shirts from the dresser. Sliding it over my head, I felt the cool cotton caress my skin. Sliding into the rumpled sheets, I found the remote and was happy when I clicked the button and saw that Phantom set up the cable already. Going to ABC and pressing look back, I started watching *Modern Family* again, only this time uninterrupted. I felt so relaxed and comfortable. *I think this is the least stressed I have been in a long time.* I could feel my baby girl kicking me like she agreed with me. The only thing that would have made this evening better was some food. *I am starving, but I am sure there is no food in this empty house.*

Hearing the door downstairs click and the alarm chirp, I knew it was him before I even heard his heavy footsteps on the stairs. My body tingled in anticipation of seeing his sexy body and his mean eyes that went soft when he looked at me. "Hey, I brought you some snacks and some dinner so you could have a good night's sleep." He must have seen me trying to look at what he had in his hand because he told me what it was. "I got some garlic and parmesan chicken from Wings Over Rochester, with the side of cheese sauce and waffle fries. I also brought some chocolate chip cookies, Oreo ice cream with sprinkles, and a few bags of salt and vinegar chips and Cheetos so you can mix them together." He was smirking as I started tearing into my food. I was smiling like a little kid on Christmas since he got all of my favorites, and I noticed the peach tea he was holding behind his back.

"Phantom, don't play. Your daughter said she needs that tea you trying to hide. Now give it," I said, half-joking.

"Damn, Inaya, what I'ma eat, ma? You ain't even leave me a chicken bone," he said with a fake shocked look as he handed me my tea and turned around like he was leaving.

"Jah, you don't have to go. I wouldn't mind the company. And I really wanted to thank you for this house. It is everything I always wanted when I thought of the place I would be raising my children. It is perfect. Even though it is empty, I am sure that Azia will have it filled before we can blink, so make sure to hide your black card."

Walking over to me and kicking off his Timbs as he got to the bed, he climbed up and pulled me closer to him. "Inaya, you don't have to thank me. I would give you and our girls my last. I would give you whatever you want. The whole world if I could. You are the only girl I have ever fallen in love with, and I am so happy you are going to finally let me take care of you and the girls the way I should be. Hell, I didn't even know what my aunt was up to, but I am happy she said whatever she did to get you to move somewhere safe. And you better start using that damn money that is in your bank account. You have like thirty stacks in there that has been collecting interest the past few months."

Shit, I didn't even look at that bank account anymore. I went to Walmart and opened a Second Chance checking account once the bank told me we couldn't keep moving the money back and forth between our accounts. I just abandoned that one, but I still had the card somewhere. *I may need that chunk of money to furnish the house and get the kids their Christmas stuff.* "Jahdair, do you mind if I have Nadia come live here with me and the girls? I don't want her to be a burden on my grandmother, and it would be good for her. She would be in a better school district and not in the city anymore." I made sure to make the baby face where I tilted my head to the side and smiled just a little.

"Come on, now, I think it's a great idea. Get her all set up in the new school, and I will give you some bread to get her school clothes and shit. Anyway, ma, this is your crib. I can't tell you who to have up in your shit, except it better not be no nigga up in here, ever. If a dude wants to come home to you, tell his pussy ass to buy you a crib just as nice or nicer. I will kill any man you try to bring around my kids, believe that." His eyes got black when he said that. I was turned on. I loved when he was aggressive, or maybe I just really needed to fuck. Moving closer to Phantom, I ran my tongue over his lips before I stopped to slip it inside his mouth. Lifting up his red V-neck shirt, I began kissing him on his chest until I made my way down to the scar on his belly. I knew he was stabbed there when he was younger. He never told me how or why, and I never pushed him for answers. The scar was just a part of him. I loved all of him, even his imperfections.

Dipping my head lower, I began unbuckling his belt and then unbuttoning his jeans. Seeing how hard he was made me want to jump on it and ride his dick. Pulling his man out, I ran my hands over his pretty dick. The mushroom head was swollen, and his pre-cum was oozing out. Taking my tongue and licking it up, I began to circle the head gently. I was shaking. I wanted to feel him inside of me so bad.

Before I could swallow his whole dick, he pulled me up and shook his head. "Iny, you don't have to do that to me. That's not for you, ma." With that, he laid me down and took off all his clothes. Wiggling out of his T-shirt, I lay on my side and waited to feel his skin next to mine. I expected him to put me on all fours and fuck the shit out of me. Instead, his lips circled my breasts, and his hands began rubbing my clit. I was so hot, and he was fucking with me.

"Phantom, just put it in, please," I whined, begging him to give me what I wanted. Rolling on his back, he pulled me on top of him and gently inserted the tip in. I began winding on the head, trying to slam my body down on his, but he held me in a tight grip and gently dipped inside of me and then pulled out. Finally, he let go of my waist and began kissing me while grabbing my ass. I was putting in work. Feeling him swell inside me just excited me more because I knew he was about to cum and so was I.

"Damn, girl, this pussy is so good. I miss fucking this pussy," he cried out in my ear. Feeling his warm nut fill me up, I came so hard I got a cramp in my belly, and our daughter began kicking like crazy. Phantom shot up, looking crazy. "Is she okay? I didn't hurt her, did I?"

"She is good, just being busy is all. I am not in any pain, and see? She settled down as soon as she heard your voice." I lay on my side and curled up next to him, laying my hand on his heart. I felt satisfied now that I got some dick, but sad because I was alone. The man I loved wouldn't be with me but had a different girlfriend he was willing to try with. "Phantom, if you would give me the world, why wouldn't you give me you? That is all

I ever wanted." Feeling his body stiffen, I held on to him tighter because I knew he wanted to get up and leave, and I really needed him next to me, even if it was only for one night. "You know what? Never mind, it was a stupid question," I backtracked and closed my eyes, feeling the tears I tried to hold back spill onto his chest.

Chapter 10

Sahnai

I had been here, wherever here was for . . . well, shit, I had been here for a while. It was not like my kidnappers gave me a calendar or let me know what day of the week it was. I didn't even fucking know if it was night or day with this blindfold on my face. Once, she took the blindfold off. Yeah, it was a she. I would never forget that a woman was doing this to me. I could hear her voice in my nightmares. I didn't know that a woman could do these things to another woman, but I guessed payback was a bitch. I was still trying to figure out what she was paying me back for. Mostly she just rambled on about how he shouldn't have ever met me, and it was my fault he was gone. Some days she blamed my mother, but that made no sense since my mother had been dead for a while. Yesterday, I finally lost it and screamed that maybe it was a good thing he left her, even if it was because I fucked him, because she was a crazy bitch. After mumbling that this was why men cheated, she took a hanger and beat me with it, then used the triangular corner to fuck me with it.

I could hear her tell a man that he was sick. I knew who she was talking to because I could smell him in the room. He always wore cheap-ass cologne. It was Honest. All along he had been here, and as soon as the lady left, he was in the room, washing me up and fucking me in any hole he could fit his tiny dick in. He usually professed his love and said how sorry he was. Opening my eyes and squishing my face so I could see out of one corner of the blindfold, I decided to try to peek at what the hell was going on. While she was fucking me with the pink plastic hanger and rubbing her breasts, Honest stood close to me on the bed, jacking his dick. He had his face looking up at the ceiling with his eyes closed in ecstasy. I took a few seconds to look at the face of the lady torturing me. Her face was a pretty caramel, and she had long red hair. It looked like a weave and was pulled back into a slick ponytail. She looked like she was in her late forties or early fifties, and her facial features kind of resembled Honest's. She was very thin and had small, dried-up breasts that looked like two raisins. *I bet this ho is on drugs or something, because she sure looks like a crackhead, even though she has a pretty face.*

I had done a lot of shit to people, but how the fuck did this shit happen to me? I had tried to figure this out for a while now, days, maybe weeks now. She said I made him kill himself, so it couldn't be about Honest. I actually didn't do him wrong. I was just into his money more than him. Feeling a hot sensation in my private area and then tingling, I began to scream out in agony. Again, this lady made her way down and began licking my pussy while playing with hers. I didn't understand what her problem was. *Does she hate me, love me, or want to fuck me?* I didn't remember turning down any females. None I could think of had ever tried to hit on me. *She is insane.* A few days ago, after she used a dildo to fuck me and herself, she put my feet in buckets of cold ice water and left me tied to a chair. I was left like that the whole night. I couldn't help but pee myself because it was so cold. I couldn't feel my feet after a while, and I just knew I was going to die from hypothermia. She left me sitting in my own piss, shivering and suffering for days. The smell was so terrible I gagged every time I took too deep of a breath.

I could no longer cry because this must be what I deserved. I had been terrible to everyone I ever met, even the one man I ever loved, and that was Lox. It started when I was a kid. I knew my mom wasn't shit as long as I could remember. This caused me to develop a lot of hate and jealousy in my heart. The first person I was ever jealous of was my little cousin, Inaya. When Inaya was born, she was loved by everyone except her mother. There was just something about her light skin and her pretty brown eyes that made people's hearts melt when they saw her. But not for my aunt. I remembered so many times her mom would beat her and belittle her and treat her like shit and when it happened, I would feel so much joy inside. I was happy that she was no longer the perfect little girl in the family. Her looks and cute smile could not save her. In those moments, she became more like me, and it made me feel good, like I could feel my soul smile. I would lie and let her take the blame for stuff I did like breaking glasses, making a mess, or even stealing stuff. Only thing was, my grandma always knew it was me. She could read me like a book.

I wished I could say that was where it ended, but nope. This childhood behavior was just the beginning. I remembered one thing Inaya always talked about was how she wanted at least one of her parents to love her, and since we all knew it was not her mother, she was always looking for an unknown father who would show her all the love she missed. Hell, I could relate because I was always looking out the window, hoping some unknown dad would come and save me from being an unwanted orphan. When I was twelve, I heard my aunt and grandmother arguing about Inaya's father. All along, he loved her. He wanted to be in her life, but my aunt wouldn't let him. When she was a baby, he was a part of her life until he dumped my aunt because he saw the way she was treating Inaya. He tried to get custody, but back then, it was harder for men to take custody of little girls, so he was shut down in court and shut out of her life forever. That day, they found out her dad had died from a car accident, and our grandmother wanted to tell Inaya and show her the cards and letters her father had written her, but her mother said no.

I could have told her. Hell, I should have told her, but why should she have a father who loved her and wanted her even if he was dead when I had no one? All I had was a dead mother and an unknown father. So all these years, I kept it to myself, silently laughing every time my little cousin cried about not having a parent who loved her. I always offered her comfort, though. I was not evil. Well, at least I didn't think so. Then there was Noah. Yes, Kadia's father was a nigga I used to fuck at one point. It was all about money and control. This was before Kadia, but not before Inaya had become a part of his life. I didn't want my cousin having anything better than me, and at that point, I couldn't get a boyfriend because I had a reputation of being a pop off at a young age. One of the reasons I had to move to another state was because of that reputation. That and the fact that that nigga's money was longer in other places. I had always been all about the money.

Trying to think of all the men I hooked up with, stole shit from, or let spoil me until they fell off or got knocked was making my brain hurt. When the money stopped, so did I, and I was pretty sure I left a trail of broken hearts along the way. I was trying to remember if any of them looked like Honest or his creepy-ass mammy or whoever she was. I never heard him call her his mom, so I wondered if she was an aunt or cousin. Today felt different from the rest of the days I was here. I woke up a while ago, and I could tell it was morning because I could see the brightness even through my blindfold. My hands and wrists ached from being tied up and immobile for so long. My legs felt weak, and my hips hurt from lying on this bed. The only movement they got was when I was being molested or raped.

Hearing voices in the hallway, my heart began beating fast, and all I could hear was the loud thump, thump, thump, until I took a few deep breaths and tried to calm myself down. I swore I heard the lady say something about today being the day I would finally die. With all the bad I had done, I did one thing right, and that was my baby. I couldn't allow these people to kill me. *I have a son who needs me. I love li'l Q more than anything.* I still remembered the day he was born. He came out looking just like his father, eating like his greedy behind, too. But his smile was all me. He was the one person who brought me constant joy, and I was going home to him somehow. I had to find a way back to him. All kids need their mom, and I needed to be a better person for him.

"Nah, we're not killing shawty on my watch. Why did you take her if your plan was just to kill her?" I heard Honest ask her with venom in his voice. He sounded truly hurt, and I wondered if he really loved me but was just scared of her, or did he think he would get to keep me when she was done playing her sick games?

"Honest, listen, son. I don't understand the sick obsession you have with her. You understand that even if I wasn't killing her, if the kidnapping never happened, you and Sahnai could never be together, right? I mean, there are laws against that kind of stuff, and I need you to get your head in the game and out of the clouds. If I had known you were going to be such a pussy, I would not have asked for any help from you. I mean, damn, he was your father too, and you should want her to get everything she deserves. She is the reason your father is dead. She is the reason me and him broke up and our marriage was ruined. Some days I wonder whose child you are. It's like I birthed an idiot," she ranted on and on.

Now I am really lost. How can me and Honest being together be illegal? Does his mom mean the rape? That would make sense, but how did I kill his father? I didn't know who the hell his father was. I didn't remember ever meeting him. Feeling the breeze from the hallway let me know the door was open. I knew it was Honest again because I could smell his Curve cologne and the faint smell of liquor and weed. Honest was a huge smoker and drinker. I guessed I saw why. If Miss Crazy were my mom, I would be trying to drink my troubles away too.

I felt his hot breath on my cheek, and he whispered in my ear, "Don't worry, my love, I will not let her kill you. I am going to get you out of here, and then we will be able to be together finally, just me and you. I can't wait until you have my babies, and we can get married. I will give you anything you want. I love you, Sahnai."

Hearing the echo of her shoes as she rushed across the room, I heard a thump. I guessed she pushed Honest's ass to the side or something. I was being sat in an upright position, and then the blindfold was snatched from my face. "Little girl, you don't remember me, do you? I can see you are still confused about what this is all about. When you had sex with my husband and my son, you never noticed a resemblance? Nothing looked familiar?" She screamed her questions at me.

I just shook my head because I had no fucking clue what she meant. I guessed if I fucked father and son, I should have seen some type of resemblance, but fuck it, I didn't. Maybe that wasn't even his daddy. *She could be over here lying and shit.*

"First, your funky-ass dopefiend mother, Monica, ruined my life. The day you were born, my life crumbled. Yeah, your daddy wanted to be with you, wanted me to take you into our home to live with my sweet son. I thought when I killed your mother it was over, the problem was fixed."

I could feel my mouth hanging wide open as the rage was coursing through my body at what she just said to me. She killed my mother? We were told it was a drug overdose. I didn't know if I should try to whoop her ass even though I was still tied up, or look around for a camera crew, because I swore I was being "punk'd."

"Oh, you little home-wrecker, you look so confused. Didn't your mammy ever tell you that you had a daddy? Or maybe you remember your daddy better as Junior. Yeah, I can see by the look on your face you remember Junior." Her voice began to fade into the background as visions of Junior flashed before my eyes. I met Junior right before I left to move to Brooklyn. I was still a teenager, about 17 years old, and he was at least twice my age. Hell, I never stopped to ask. I could see his face like he was standing next to me. Probably because as soon as I remembered him, I realized he looked like Honest. I was fucking Honest's father. Junior was my first big come-up. I knew he loved me. He always told me I reminded him of someone, someone he once loved. He gave me thousands of dollars, jewelry, and even my first car. I never took him for a drug dealer. He was clean-cut, wore khaki pants, button-down shirts, and even ties. Sometimes I even noticed a briefcase in his car when he would come to pick me up.

"Nothing to say? Does the cat have your tongue? Do you understand what you did to my husband? To my son? Junior was your father! You had sex with your father. He took all of our money and spent it on you. He cashed in his 401(k) to buy your ho ass a new car while me and his son rode around in a broke-down Honda. He fell in love with you because you reminded him of your mother, and when he found out who you were, he couldn't live with himself. One day, he went to pick you up from your house, and when you came out and called to your grandmother, he realized who you were. That was when he stopped messing with you. He lost his mind. He came home one day and began drinking and beating on me and Honest because he was sickened by what he had done."

Everything she said was true. I slept with my father. *What kind of sick person am I?* Further realization hit as I thought about me and Honest and all I had done with him. I fucked my own brother, my blood brother I never knew I had. Feeling the sour bile rise in my throat, I began to vomit violently. I couldn't stop. Even though my life was in danger, all I could think about was the disgusting thing I had done. "God, I didn't know. How could I have known? I am so sorry, God. Why am I always being punished?" I sobbed out loud.

"You could have known. You should have at least known that he was married. I know you saw the ring on his finger. You should have left other people's husbands alone. All you saw was dollar signs, and guess what? Him being your father, the father you always wanted, I am sure is karma. You are receiving the ultimate payback for what you have done. Your father couldn't handle the fact that he molested his own child, so after months of drinking himself into a depression, he came home one day, found his old shotgun, and sat at our kitchen table. He didn't even leave a note, just sat down with a picture of you in front of him and tears in his eyes, and then he blew his brains out." With the last statement, she pulled a shotgun from behind her and pointed it in my direction.

I began to tremble and shift my eyes around the bare room, trying to find a way out of this prison before I ended up dead like my father. I was still emotionally trying to get myself together, but I really didn't have time for this. In a flash, Honest jumped up from the chair he was sitting in and hit his mother in the head with a small figurine. Blood began spewing out of her head, and she dropped to the ground. As he grabbed me in his arms and ran out of the room, I noticed his mother was still breathing. Seeing the sick grin on Honest's face, I realized I was going from one unstable situation to another. I was being kidnapped by my ex-boyfriend/brother who wanted me to marry him and have his babies. I didn't know if I should laugh or cry as I watched the sun disappear and the trunk of Honest's car close over my face.

Chapter 11

Inaya

Rolling over onto my left side, I could feel my baby going crazy, kicking me in my bladder. I should have known this baby would give me hell. "Okay, Mommy is getting up, don't be mean. Sheesh," I murmured while rubbing my belly, trying to calm her down. I swore she wanted me to spank her behind the day she was born with all the nonsense she kept up.

Now that I was over the morning sickness, I wanted to eat everything all day long, and when my daughter was hungry, she acted a straight-up fool. I was off for two weeks, since Christmas was coming in less than five days, and I had a baby shower to get ready for in less than a month. I was happy to get it out of the way since I was due March twenty-fifth. I liked to be organized, so I would be able to have all the baby's items purchased and set up.

I was excited about this holiday. This was the first Christmas I could ever remember that I was looking forward to the day. I finally had a family to share it with, people who loved me and who were there for me. *I may not have the man I love, but I have decided to pray on it. Maybe things can change. I cannot give up hope. Why would God bring this man in my life who changed things so much for me for the better, and then not allow us to work out? God wouldn't do that to me.*

Taking out the maple bacon, eggs, butter, and cheese, I decided to make bacon and cheesy eggs. Humming "Silent Night," I made my way around the island, picking up crayons that Vivy and Kadia left out while doing homework last night. I did move into the new house right after Thanksgiving, and I was so thankful to Aunt Sena for talking sense into me.

I loved the house, and with Azia's shopping bug and Phantom's money, the new furniture looked amazing. I even got all new kitchen stuff. Instead of the girly colors, I was using square-shaped dishes in all white and all teal, and gray accessories. It matched well with the stainless-steel appliances and the gray tiles on the floor and backsplash. Nadia had been with me since then, and even though my grandmother didn't admit it, she seemed very grateful to have that responsibility taken off of her shoulders. I got my cousin into the middle school out here. It was one of the top five schools in the state. She joined the indoor track team and the debate team and a whole bunch of clubs. She seemed so happy and grateful. She thanked me like five times a day.

Hearing the door chirp, I assumed it was one of the girls because we were going to finish Christmas shopping and buying decorations for the baby shower. Smelling him before I saw him, I realized it was Phantom creeping in the house. Since I moved in, he came and went a lot, stopping by at odd times of the night to crawl into bed with me and just hold me. He would not give me the dick no matter how I tried. I had been sleeping butt-ass naked and everything, but he had not given in. When I asked him about it or said slick shit like "Why aren't you with your girl," he said he was spending time with his kids.

Feeling his strong arms wrap around my waist, his hand crept around to rub my belly. Running my hand over his, tracing the dragon tattoo up his arm, I relaxed my body into his.

"Ma, you waited too long to feed my baby this morning. That's why she in there kicking yo ass and shit," he said with a laugh. I was not as amused.

"Your daughter is getting her ass whooped if she doesn't cut the bullshit," I shot back at him. Finally, my food was done, and I sat at the island to eat. Being nice, I made Phantom a plate of food and a cup of tea. "So what's up? You know I am leaving soon. What brings you by?" I asked with a slight attitude.

Throwing a stack of money on the countertop next to me, he smirked my way. He had gotten good at handling my little attitudes lately.

"Just bringing you some money to do what you want while you out shopping." He bent down to kiss my lips, and I couldn't even think of a smart-ass response. I just threw the money in my bag and stood up to get ready.

Hearing the girls downstairs talking shit to Phantom, I hurried into another pair of thick tights. This time, they were dark brown, and I paired them with a cream Pink sweater with sparkly gold writing. Stuffing my swollen feet into a pair of brown and gold sparkly Uggs, I was ready. I couldn't wait to wear jeans and dresses and normal-people clothes again. I was tired of sweats and tights. "Let's go, ladies," I called out as I got to the bottom stair and almost lost my balance. Three pairs of hands leaped up to steady me. Rolling my eyes, I let them know I was okay. "Azia, my car or yours?" I asked as we headed out front.

Seeing Alani's face scrunch up, she said, "Why don't we ever take my car?"

Looking at Azia, I looked back at Alani. "Girl, I cannot fit in that little-ass economy car. It's cute and all, but we need you to allow Lox to cop you some new shit. You can't even fit more than two of the kids at a time," I joked, but was a little serious. "Anyway, we need the truck today since we are buying a lot of stuff. I was going to say we need two vehicles with the last-minute shopping, but I will make one of the boys pick up the packages from the first half of the trip," Azia reasoned as we stepped into her Porsche truck.

Closing my eyes until we got to the mall, all I could think about was Phantom's dick and one of those Auntie Anne's pretzels. This pregnancy shit was no joke. I was craving everything. Feeling my iPhone buzz in my purse. I pulled it out and saw a message from Phantom.

Baby Daddy: No kiss goodbye?

I responded by taking a picture of me making a kissy face and sending it. Phantom sent back a kissy emoji. *I wonder which one of the kids taught him how to use emojis.* Pulling up to the mall, I was speed walking to get me two pretzels and flavored lemonade. Ignoring the laughter of my sisters, I tore them shits up first.

"Okay, we need to go into Party City first and get the rest of the decorations for the shower," directed our shopping coach aka Azia. Following along behind her, we each got a cart and began grabbing stuff. I was having a royal baby shower, a pink and gold princess one, and even though a party planner and decorator were hired, Azia still went overboard. Next, we spent almost $600 on body sprays, perfumes, and lotions at Victoria's Secret for giveaways. I was beginning to wonder if we were doing too much for a baby shower. I was having fun, and I didn't have one with Kadia, so I decided to just let go of any negative feelings.

After filling the car with baby shower items, we went back in to finish up Christmas shopping. The kids had all of their stuff since we hit Toys "R" Us and Walmart on Black Friday. I just had to find stuff for Phantom and the girls as well as Phantom's grandmother, who was visiting us for the holiday and his aunt. Deciding on Lord & Taylor first, we all spread out, and I started out with Alani. She dressed up for work so much, I thought it would be nice to get her something cute to wear out and have fun. Seeing a pink silk scarf, I got that for her to wear to the office, and then I found a sexy white and gray dress. I thought her breasts would really pop in this dress, and she could wear it when we went out. Grabbing some new MK and Louie bags, I was almost finished, or so I thought. A few hours and three stores later, I had so many bags I had to rent a stroller to put them in.

"Oh, my God, I created a shopping monster," laughed Azia as we all met up at the food court. My baby was not missing one meal or snack. "Don't worry. Phantom is coming to get all this shit. He does have his little side piece with him, so don't get upset," she warned me.

I was good. I didn't even get worked up about Tamia and Phantom. He had to do what was best for him. As long as the kids were straight, I didn't care. At least that was what I kept telling myself. Settling in at a table with some orange chicken, shrimp fried rice, and a side of vegetables, I looked up when I heard her annoying-ass voice.

"Phantom, I could use some money to buy some Christmas gifts. That is what a boyfriend should do. I am not asking for much, just a few hundred dollars, and I never asked you for money before," Tamia whined as they made their way to our table. I could see the glint in Azia's eyes, and I knew she was about to make it clear where Phantom's money went.

Not responding to Tamia and her tantrum, Phantom made his way to us. He began picking up bags and boxes. "You were balling out, huh, Iny?" He laughed at all the shit I had.

"Hey, when you give, I spend," I said, smirking Tamia's way. Leaning down to kiss all of us on the cheeks,

Phantom grabbed the bags and was gone with his girl trailing behind, looking crushed.

"Inaya, I know you think Phantom doesn't love your ass anymore, but, girl, you got him wide open. I remember the old Phantom, and his ass was not giving any girl shit—money, the time of the day, nothing. When he used to hang with Travis, I used to hate when he came around. He was so fucking disrespectful. You changed him, made him less bitter and hateful." Alani started telling me stories of how Phantom used to embarrass girls in front of everyone in the hood. I was happy he didn't do me that way. Damn, he was mean.

Phantom

Today was the day of the baby shower, and for whatever reason, a nigga was excited. I knew it was some girl shit, but Inaya's excitement was rubbing off on me. I stayed at the house last night and finally gave baby girl the dick she'd been craving. I didn't want her miserable on her special day. My grandmother had been here since Christmas, but she was staying with my Aunt Sena for this week. Christmas was . . . hell, it was the best a nigga ever had. Inaya baked cookies and cakes with the kids for two days before, and she bought a nigga some really nice gifts. As always, she was there looking out for me when all the other bitches in my life just wanted shit. I gave Tamia a $200 gift card to some spa, and she fell in love with the kid all over again but didn't even get me a card or anything. *I am sorry, but pussy is not a gift.* A nigga was getting that anyway. Now Inaya gave me colognes, clothes, shades, and a bracelet that had to have cost her a chunk of her savings. I knew the diamonds were real by the way they shone when the sun hit. I was wearing it now.

I made sure my baby mom was straight too. I got her purses, shoes, and a diamond necklace from Kay and had them inscribe "Phantom Loves Inaya" on the back. She cried all over when she opened that one. Finally, Alani got a new whip so we could retire the Chevy Cruz. Lox got her a brand-new Lincoln MKZ. She wanted to decline the gift, but he talked her down when he told her the kids would all fit in the truck and the girls pointed out how cute it was.

Jumping up to get ready, I laid out the outfit I bought for Inaya to wear today. I knew she was going to try to throw on a pair of tights and a sweater, but I wanted her to feel good on her special day. I even hired a photographer to take family pictures of me, her, and Kadia. I got her a form-fitting dress from Bebe. That was her favorite store. It was white with black stripes outlining the ruffles that ran down the front. It was short and would only reach the tops of her knees, and she had white and silver shoes to match. I also put out some sparkly sandals for when her feet got tired from the heels. Deciding to leave a note, I just scribbled a quick "This is for you" with a heart and got out of there. I was, of course, matching her fly with all-white jeans from Buffalo and a black V-neck sweater from Versace. I threw on some black Versace shoes to match and ran my hand over my freshly done braids.

Inaya

Pulling up to Mario's, I couldn't help the butterflies in my stomach as I walked through the snow in my boots. I was carrying the gorgeous shoes that Phantom bought me so I could put them on as soon as we got inside. Alani opened the door for me, and I almost passed out.

It was so pretty. There were gold and pink streamers hanging from the ceiling and balloons in the shapes of baby bottles and rattles. Each table had pink crowns with gold accents in the middle, and the candy table looked too amazing to even touch. The pink candy apples shimmered with gold sparkles or gold lines depending on which ones they were. I was led to the front of the room where two king and queen chairs sat, and Phantom was already waiting for me to sit next to him.

Smoothing my curls behind my ear, I sat down to fix my shoes and make my way to the front. Sitting down next to Phantom, I was surprised at how many people showed up to help us celebrate our baby. The gift table looked like it was going to break under the weight of the presents. Once the DJ began playing the music and the rum punch was being served, everyone was having a good time. "Hey, come here, let's take these pictures, babe," Phantom called to me as he motioned for me to follow him to a corner with a backdrop set up. Seeing he was carrying Kadia in her matching white ruffled dress and little shiny black Mary Janes, I was holding back tears. I didn't want my makeup to get ruined before we started.

"Ma'am, look this way. Sir, put your hand on her belly and look into her eyes," the cameraman instructed.

My smile changed as Phantom looked into my eyes. I felt like I was falling in love all over again. I could feel his minty breath on my face and his heart beating as he sat close to me. His eyes were telling me that he loved me more than anything.

"Wow, that was amazing. These photos will be great, and I will have everything ready by the end of the week. I am going to take some pictures of the cakes and gifts before you start opening gifts," the photographer said, interrupting our moment.

"Mommy, can we open my sister's presents now, please?" asked Kadia while holding hands with me and Phantom.

"Sure, baby, let's get to it. I need your help because there are so many," I replied. That was an understatement. There was a ton of shit. Did people really buy big-ass gifts like this for other people? I assumed Azia and Alani would buy everything on the registry and my guests would bring small gifts like clothes or bibs. Our daughter got almost two of everything. There were cases of diapers, Pack 'n Plays, swings, clothes and more clothes, and the stroller I fell in love with: a white and pink Quinny. It was amazing, and I should have known Azia would be the one to get it. *Now, I just have to figure out how to fold it down.* By the time we got to the cake, I was walking around barefoot and ready for a nap.

Seeing Phantom and Lox's grandmother headed my way, I slowed down so I could speak to her. "Good evening, Mama. Are you doing okay?" I greeted her politely.

"Inaya, I want to tell you that our family is so blessed to have you. I know that grandson of mine says he has a girlfriend. Huh, that one is trash, but you have his heart. I have known him his whole life, watched him grow and seen the damage his mother caused. He has never loved anyone the way he has loved you. I want you to have this as a gift. It is not expensive, but it was my wedding ring. My husband and I were married for forty years before he passed away. This ring was his mother's ring before mine. It has meaning." She handed me a pretty silver ring with a single diamond. I loved it, and of course, the hormones had me gone, and I began to hug her and cry uncontrollably.

"All right, Mama, why is she crying like that? I think In-aya needs to get home. It has been a long day," Phantom instructed, pulling me close to him and trying to lead me to the door. The DJ began playing this song I loved by Charlie Puth, called "One Call Away."

"Phantom, wait until this song is over, please?" I asked in my best little-girl voice. Surprisingly, he turned to face me and pulled me in his arms, and then he began to dance with me in the middle of the room. Not wanting to ruin the moment, I didn't comment on the fact that he was singing the song off-key in my ears. If I could have stayed in this moment for the rest of my life, I would have. Letting my head drop to his shoulder, I felt my eyes start to close even though my body was still moving with his.

"Okay, Iny, it's time to go, princess." With that, he picked me up and carried me to the car. *Damn, I love a strong man. I hope he gives me the D again,* was all I could think as I felt him start the truck and drive away.

Waking up the next morning, I was still in a great mood until I realized that Sahnai didn't even come to my baby shower. No call, gift, or anything. I made sure I sent an invitation to her house, and it didn't come back returned. Phantom told me she was just being a bitch, and that was why she skipped Christmas, but I was starting to wonder if something else was going on. Throwing on my gray sweatsuit and some slippers with rubber bottoms, I grabbed my bag and jumped in the Audi.

Pulling up to the house, I could tell something was off. Mail was all on the front porch and leaking out of the mailbox. Did my cousin leave town and not tell anyone? I just couldn't see her doing that to li'l Q. Walking up the steps carefully, I went to knock on the door, and it flew open. *What the fuck?* She would never leave her door unlocked and opened. I noticed the Louie Vuitton luggage piled by the front door, and my stomach tied in knots. "Sahnai, are you here?" I called out. Not hearing anything, I walked through the house and found nothing. No one was there, and her car was still in the driveway. As I sat down at the kitchen table, my foot stepped in something sticky. Looking down, I saw the snow from my shoes mixed with dried red stuff on the floor. *Oh, my God, it's blood.*

Something happened to my cousin here. I can feel it. Why is there a puddle of blood on the kitchen floor? Noticing her cell phone on the floor under the kitchen counter and her purse on top of her luggage, I felt my heart start to race. Who leaves home with no phone and no handbag? Nothing, just herself. My hands were shaking as I called Phantom for help. I prayed he picked up fast because I felt like I was going to be sick or pass out, and suddenly, I felt sharp pains in my belly.

Phantom

Watching *SportsCenter* at Tamia's house, I let my mind wander to the girl I really wanted to be with, Inaya. She looked so pretty yesterday at the baby shower. I would have gladly fucked her to sleep last night, except she fell asleep long before we made it home. Maybe today I would go over and make love to her. Tamia kept walking by me in some little-ass shorts and a sports bra, but I was not turned on. I was getting tired of whatever this shit was with her. She was supposed to just be someone to do, not someone I was with permanently. My phone rang, and I was glad for the distraction. Seeing Inaya's face flash on the screen, I couldn't help my smile. "Hey, Iny, what's up?" I asked.

"Jahdair, help me, she is dead. I don't know what to do. Why didn't we check on her? Arghhhh, I am in so much pain. Please come and get me. Help me find her. I should have checked on her," she sobbed into the phone. She was crying so hard I could barely get her to tell me where she was.

Jumping up and running out the front door, I ignored Tamia's cries asking where I was going. I made it across town to Sahnai's house in fifteen minutes. I was running red lights and all. I picked up my business phone and dialed Lox because I didn't want to hang up with Inaya.

"Son, get to Sahnai's crib now. Something has gone wrong, and Iny is over there freaking out." I gave the order to my cousin, then threw down my phone. I knew he would come.

Pulling up and grabbing my nine from under the seat, I slowly walked to the door. "Inaya, I am here. Are you alone?" I asked as I crept to the front door. Before I could react, it was flung open, and Inaya was there bent over in pain.

"Jah, I am having the baby. It's too early for her to come. Why is this happening to me?" she wailed as I grabbed her in my arms. Not wasting any more time on her cousin's house or situation, I got my girl into the car and raced to the hospital. Lox could handle the Sahnai situation once he got there.

Pulling up to the emergency lane at Highland Hospital, I grabbed the first nurse I saw walking by. "Help! My wife is only seven months pregnant, and she is in so much pain she thinks she is having the baby!" I yelled, grabbing her arm. After that, shit happened really fast. Inaya was rushed inside in a wheelchair and then taken to the back. After a ton of paperwork, I ran back there to be with her but was stopped by the doctor outside of her door.

"Sir, your wife and baby are in danger, and we have to do an emergency C-section right away or we can lose them both. If you want to be in there, meet me at the end of the hall and change into the blue sterile outfit the nurse has waiting."

I didn't wait for him to finish. I ran to the nurse and threw on all the shit she had waiting for me. I could feel my heart racing and my palms sweating. For once, I couldn't control a situation. This was not an enemy I could kill or get rid of. I couldn't keep the woman I loved safe at all. I couldn't protect my daughter, and I may lose another one.

I held Inaya's hand once they wheeled her in, and she looked at me with her big brown eyes, scared. "Jahdair, if I don't make it, I love you. I have never stopped loving you, and please take care of Kadia. Jah, make sure they save our baby," she whispered as they put the gas mask over her face. Leaning down to whisper in her ear, I didn't know what to say because for the first time in my life, I was scared.

"I love you too, Iny. You're gonna be all right." Suddenly, a bunch of alarms started going off, and then I heard "Code blue." I thought they forgot I was in the room because no one asked me to leave, but I felt like I shouldn't have been there. Seeing them pull my baby girl out and run her to the side, I felt tears fall from my eyes. She was so small, and I didn't hear her crying like babies should. At least, I thought they should. When my sister had the twins, I was there, and both of them cried right away.

Suddenly, I was being asked to leave. "Sir, we need you to leave now. You can go meet your daughter in the nursery, and the doctors will speak to you about her status," one of the doctors said while almost shoving me out the door. Slowly, I walked to the nursery. I didn't want to leave Inaya's side, but I had to be strong and go see about our baby.

"Hello, I am here to check on my daughter. She was just born and is two months early." My voice shook a little when I asked the nurse about her.

"Sir, what is the mother's last name?" she asked. At that moment, I felt ashamed. *Inaya's last name should be Lucas*. I should have made her my wife instead of leaving her to be another baby mama.

"The last name is Walker."

She moved to look on the computer and checked, I guessed. A few minutes later, she looked at me with sympathy on her face. *God, please let my baby be okay. I know I have lived a fucked-up life, but don't punish my kids.* All I could do was say a silent prayer in my head.

"Sir, your daughter is doing well. She was small, only four pounds, but for being born so early, she is actually a great size. We are keeping her in the NICU for a while until we are sure she is breathing and eating on her own, but you can come see her," she told me, turning to open the door to my left. Walking in, I was a wreck because I didn't know if I should be happy about my daughter or worried about Inaya. "Wash your hands here," the nurse instructed, showing me a huge sink. Washing my hands for a few minutes, I then followed her into a room with tiny cribs with clear coverings. Sitting down next to the one labeled "Baby Walker," I saw the most amazing sight before me.

Our daughter was lying in the crib, crying her little eyes out, looking just like her mama when she cried. The only thing the baby had from me was her cocoa skin tone and her dark eyes. She had her mother's nose and ears and even her tiny little lips. As soon as they placed the baby in my arms, I felt a feeling I never felt before. I was really in here feeling like a bitch-ass nigga, soft like a damn marshmallow and shit. She stopped crying as soon as I held her close, and I just sat there rocking her back and forth in the chair. I couldn't do anything or go anywhere until I knew Inaya was okay. Hours later, a doctor finally came and found me.

"Sir, your wife made it through the second surgery. At first, she was bleeding out and we didn't think she would make it, but she is a fighter. You can go see her for a little while if you want, but then she needs to rest."

A few days later, I sat watching Inaya hold our daughter, and I knew that she was the one. She had always been the one since the first day I saw her. My heart knew then. I could still see her in my mind. I had just moved in and was looking out the window, and she was struggling. Kades was in her arms, and her big-ass bag with schoolbooks was on her back. She looked up at me like she could feel my eyes on her, but she couldn't see me. That was when Kadia shifted in her arms, and she stopped to settle her. Even though she looked defeated when she walked up at that moment, she smiled as she looked down at her daughter and gave her a kiss. At that moment, my heart fell in love with her.

Now my mind took a lot longer. I judged Iny, cheated on her, and abandoned her. But now my mind had come to terms with the fact that there was no one else for me. Inaya almost died having our baby and then suffered a lot of pain after, but she never complained. Even when our daughter almost cost her her life, her only concern was for our baby and if she would be okay. I was getting my girl back whether she knew it or not.

Kahnai Kassandra Lucas was a daddy's girl already. Inaya decided to give our daughter the middle name Kassandra to honor my first child. That was the kind of shit I meant. Baby girl was so kind. Gently placing a kiss on her and Kahnai's foreheads, I spoke in a low tone. "Babes, I will be right back. I'ma go grab Kadia to come see you both." This caused her to smile, and she nodded.

As I walked toward the elevator, my phone was blowing up. *What now? Like I almost just lost my girl and
baby. I can't deal with any more bullshit.* Seeing Tamia's
name flash across the screen, I wanted to throw the
phone out of the window. *This bitch knows I am up here
on some emergency-type shit, yet here she goes, blowing me the fuck up. I gotta get my shit together and stop
fucking with this broad.*

Chapter 12

Lox

Every time I looked around, my life was filled with chaos. After finding out what we did when Inaya went to look for Sahnai, I felt more than anger and stress. I felt guilt. It didn't mean I wanted to be with her, but it meant I felt bad for not thinking to check on her. Never did I go to the house and think something might be wrong or she was in some kind of danger. This shit could be about me for all I knew. I was a drug dealer. I murdered people for a living. Some got shot or stabbed, and some died a slower death with the drugs I served them. I should have known something was up. Hell, someone could be after my kids if they took Sahnai. Maybe they were there looking for Q or even me.

Between Inaya having the baby early and Alani acting more than strange lately, I had been running back and forth to the hospital with Aiden. He was always sick, and I was tired of seeing my baby suffer. I was hoping they figured this shit out soon because he was in pain, and I knew he was being well taken care of, so it was not something I was doing. Calling a few people I knew out of town, I felt like I could do no more at the moment to find

Sahnai. I was going to try everything I could. It didn't seem like she was dead, from the little bit of blood we found in the house. I put some money out there for that nigga Honest, because I really felt like he was the key to all of this shit.

I sat in the crib and held Aiden. Suddenly, he began to choke, and his body started shaking. *What the fuck is happening?* I didn't know what to do, but I thanked God that Miss Wanda was there, because she jumped into action. I called an ambulance, and the fire department was at my door in a matter of minutes. They put the oxygen mask on my little man, and the ambulance rushed him to Strong Hospital. I rode in the back the whole time, praying he would be okay. I tried to find his mother the other day to ask her about his medical history, her pregnancy, anything that could help us figure out why he was so sick. All I found when I did catch up with her was a shell of Toya. She was high off of something and walking down Lyell Avenue looking for her next hit. I wished I had it in me to help her, but I didn't, so I left her where she was.

After agreeing to have my blood drawn, I sat there waiting to hear anything. I knew my baby was stable, but still, I needed to know what was wrong with him. I texted the family, letting them know what was going on and where I was. Feeling her presence before she sat down, I knew Alani had come to check on me, or maybe it was just to check on Aiden. Shit, I didn't care. I was happy she was here. "Thanks," was all I said as she sat down and put her arms around me. Finally, after hours of waiting, a team of doctors walked out to speak with us.

"Mr. Hall, we need to speak to you about your son." It took me a few seconds to realize they were waiting for

Alani to leave. As soon as she shifted to get up, I held her next to me with a forceful grip.

"This is Aiden's stepmother, so anything you need to tell us, just go ahead."

"Well, there are a few things. First of all, we have found the cause of all of Aiden's issues. He has cystic fibrosis. This is when the body cannot break down certain enzymes and causes the body to become weak and the immune system to be compromised. We have a specialist here who will walk you through the disease and how to manage it so Aiden can have a long, healthy life. Now as for the other thing . . ." The doctor kind of shifted and looked uncomfortable as he continued. "We did some testing since Aiden has a genetic condition, and even though you are related, I am sorry to inform you that you are not Aiden's biological father. I mean, sir, your name is on the birth certificate, and he is in your care, so it is not my business, but it is my job to tell you the facts."

"I would like to see him now. Thank you for the information." I stood up and shook the doctor's hand. I didn't give a fuck what any blood test said. Aiden was my son. I was the one who saved him and loved him, and it would be over my dead body that my pops or strung-out-ass Toya would ever get their hands on him. Walking into the room, I sat down on one side of the bed, and Alani sat on the other.

"Mommy and Daddy are here," she told him as she held his hand.

Finally, I got a lead on this pussy Honest. All along he was only an hour away in Buffalo, New York. I grabbed our little nigga Jrock and decided I was making moves on this cat tonight. "Son, you ready?" I asked as I pulled up in my all-black Ford Expedition. Hitting me with a head nod, he jumped in the passenger seat. That was what I loved about J. He was a quiet kid and always willing to put in work.

Pulling up to the address I was given on East Delavan, it looked like someone was home because the lights were on and a black Maxima was parked in the driveway. It was still early in the day, but fuck it, I was going in now. "Let's just kick in the front door. I need to find my baby moms, and I don't have any time to waste," I told J as we walked to the front door. Days like today I was happy I worked out and shit. Taking my right foot, I slammed my Timberland through the front door and ran in with my Glock in hand.

What I saw left me speechless. Sahnai was tied up and lying on the floor, naked, and bleeding from a cut on her head. Next to her was Honest, and he had a few holes in him that looked fresh. Standing over them was an old-ass lady with a shotgun pointed at Sahnai. "You thought you could have my son the way you had my husband? You cannot. I will kill him before you have him!" she yelled as she reloaded the gun and pointed it at Sahnai's head. She was so into what she was doing she never even heard us burst through the front door. Taking a shot, I made sure I got the old bitch right in the face, so there was no chance of her coming back to haunt me. Snatching her handbag and Sahnai, I told J to start the car so we could cut.

Just like that, Sahnai was back. Well, kind of back. I had her checked by a doctor, and she spent a few days in the hospital. The lady I killed turned out to be Honest's mother, and I didn't know who was sicker: her, Honest, or Sahnai. When I took her purse, I found a diary and a video documenting most of what she did and all of what she knew about Sahnai's ol' snake ass. I hated to be the one to tell Inaya about her father and all the shit her cousin did to her. I couldn't let her go another day feeling like the girl who was not loved by one of her parents when she truly was.

Alani

It had become so busy after I completed the $4 million project at work. I was happy to say that my company got the sale, and I got a bonus and a pat on the back from Marsha. Ever since Sahnai had been back, Lox had become even more focused on me, letting me know he saved her but wanted nothing to do with her. I was trying to trust him, but it was hard. However, I had been letting him come around and watch movies or hang out here with all the kids. Shit, being honest, I missed him, and lately I had been getting this feeling that someone was watching me, so I was not comfortable staying here alone. I hoped it was not crazy-ass Sahnai, because I didn't want to have to do her in on the strength of li'l Q and Iny. But something deep inside was telling me it was someone else. It felt like a dark cloud was following me every time I went home.

"Q, Vivy, Kadia, let's go. Time to get up. Mommy has to go to work, and Miss Wanda will be here soon." Miss Wanda was the nanny Lox used for the kids. I interviewed her and picked her out. She was a bit older and on the round side. She looked like someone's young grandmother, but not sexy. I may not have been fucking with

Lox, but I sure as hell would not invite any temptation into his home in case my love for him won over my common sense someday. I had had Q and Kadia here with me since Inaya had the baby, and Lox was still wrapping up a lot of drama on his end. Plus, he had had to almost live in the hospital with Aiden. I went up there every day to sit with Aiden. He started talking recently, and he called me Mommy. Seeing him so sick was breaking my heart, but the doctors assured us once the medicine began to take effect and his body healed, he would be like a brand-new baby. I had been seriously thinking about taking a leave of absence from my job and letting Lox financially help me so I could stay home with Aiden when he was released.

He had no other mother but me, and I didn't think a nanny should be taking care of our sick kid. "Good morning, Miss Wanda. They all ate breakfast and are ready to start their day. The girls have a field trip at school, but they have everything they need, and they will get off the bus here at the usual time. I have decided to take some time away from work starting next week so I can take care of Aiden, but we will still need you full-time, so I do not want you to worry about that," I said to our nanny with a smile. I didn't want her to feel like me staying home meant we were firing her. Not one bit. Hell, we could honestly use another one of her between Azia's boys, Nadia, and the new baby. Our family was a big one, but the kids were happy and, honestly, so was I. I just missed having Lox around. Well, I missed being in his bed and in his arms. He was still around.

"No problem. I am sure Aiden will be happy to spend more time with you and his father. Poor little guy. He is a fighter and just the sweetest baby. Well, I hope you have a good day at work. I am going to get these kids off to class." With that, she was out the door with all three kids fighting to tell her some story about vanilla cake and a tent in the living room. *I hope that happened at one of my sisters' houses. Well, Azia's house, because I know Inaya is scared of crumbs and dirt.*

Stepping into the office and asking Marsha if we could have a conversation, I sat down, hoping I wouldn't lose my job because I needed some time for my family. "Marsha, I need to ask for a short leave of absence. I just found out my stepson has cystic fibrosis, and he needs me to be home with him while he is adjusting to his medicine and rebuilds his immune system."

After a few moments of silence, she finally responded. "I respect you a lot, Alani. You are a hard worker, and I am willing to give you two months of FLMA. Please keep up with emails from home and attend the monthly meeting so you do not get behind. Also, you are caught up with your work, and as a thank-you for closing and following through on the historical home sale, you can begin your leave today, and on Friday, you are being paid a bonus from that sale."

Not wasting any time, I thanked her and made my way to my new truck. I loved the truck so much more than my car. I decided to cook Lox a nice dinner and invite him over so I could tell him the good news. As soon as I pulled into Walmart, I began feeling like someone was watching me again. Looking around, everything seemed okay. Nothing was out of place.

Grabbing something from every aisle, I went to the checkout with a full cart. *Damn, I came in here for veggies and a steak, and I ended up with half the store.* After paying the cashier, I made my way to the car.

"Alani, I want to see my fucking daughter," said a deep voice close to my ear. I already knew it was Ray. I bet he was the one following me, trying to get close to Vivy.

"Ray, for the last time, me and you were a one-night thing, and I promise she is not your daughter. She is Travis's. Now, please, leave me alone," I said in a controlled tone, even though I was shaking inside.

"Alani, I meant what I said. I will be back around again, and she'd better be there," he threatened before he slowly walked away.

Knowing I really needed to tell Lox what was going on, I was dreading this conversation. I had not wanted to reveal this secret to anyone, definitely not Lox. I went home and put the groceries away and started cooking. Hearing the doorbell, I went to let Lox in. He was carrying a sleeping Q, and Vivy was bouncing around behind him.

"Hey, baby," I called as I gave her a hug and twirled her around.

It seemed like dinner went by too fast, because I had something to say. Vivy went to sleep right away and so did li'l Q. Any other time, their asses would have been running around asking for another story or a drink.

Pouring myself a vodka and cranberry, I sat down next to Lox on the couch. "Babe, I need to talk to you. I know you would want me to tell you if something was going on, and something is. I've been feeling like someone has been watching me lately. I know it sounds silly, but I can just feel it. Anyway, today coming out of the store, I figured out who it was. Lox, I have to tell you something I did that I am not proud of. I cheated on Travis one night. I was angry and drunk, and I had sex with this dude from around the way named Ray. Now he is stalking me, saying Vivy is his." I could feel tears falling because Lox was looking at me with his face balled up, and he dropped my hand like he was holding hot coals.

"Yo, all I have to say is Vivy is gonna stay with me from now on until I get this handled, but, ma, you just like the rest of these bitches. I can't even believe I was running you down, trying to make you my wife." He stormed upstairs and came back down with both kids and stormed out the front door. I curled up in a ball and cried myself to sleep.

Chapter 13

Sahnai

Today Lox came to check on me. Shit, I was surprised because ever since he saved my ass and killed Mona, he acted like I had the plague. I guessed his hardheaded ass was still mad about the video I sent to his precious Alani. I mean, damn, it'd been some months, and I was kidnapped in between. *Get over it already, nigga.*

"Thanks for checking on me and for letting Azia bring the baby by yesterday. I truly missed my son. As a matter of fact, whenever you're ready, he can come back home to me. I am not injured in any way that would stop me from caring for him, so you can get a break, and he can be home," I proposed as he walked toward my front door.

"Ummm, naw, ma, he good. He is used to being with me and his brother. You need some time to relax. You need to call your cousin. She had her baby and all. Shit, if it weren't for her, we wouldn't even have known your ass was missing, and you over here treating her like she is the one who did some shit to you. Hell, your cousin kidnapped you? Or she fucked your man? Oh, the shit you think I don't know about." With that, he left me standing at the front door with my mouth wide open.

Yeah, I fucked with Noah a long time ago for some money. That was how I made it to Brooklyn in the first place. I couldn't make any excuses for that shit or any of the other things I had done out of jealousy for my cousin over the years. It really wasn't about shit but money.

As he walked down the road toward his truck, I was daydreaming about a much nicer meeting between the two of us when I saw a car come flying from out of nowhere. Watching the car speed down the street toward Lox, I screamed for him to watch out, but he couldn't hear me. He never turned around, and that meant he did not see the all-black Audi with tint racing toward him. This was all because of me. He just saved me, and he was going to die for it. The kidnapper came back to finish what she started after Honest ran off with me. All because of what I did. I never even told him what he saved me from or why. I began running from my house down the street toward his BMW, but I felt like I was in slow motion. Every step I took seemed like three steps back. Running, I tripped over a bag of leaves that someone left on their front lawn. Feeling my sweatpants rip as I hit the ground, I couldn't even focus on the pain or the blood that colored the yellow fabric as I heard the screech and crash of the all-black car as it hit the only man I ever loved. I felt the pee run down my legs as I struggled to catch my breath with the hot tears making a puddle in my mouth.

I couldn't open my eyes because I didn't want to see him like that, smooshed against the car, broken and bloody. Maybe his body flew or his head came off. I heard about that happening to a guy a while ago in a car accident. They said they found his head in a tree. I no longer wanted to run down there, and I had no strength yet, so I lay there in the road, crying.

"Sahnai, what the fuck? I just saved your ass. How you bleeding and lying in the road?" Lox said, looking down at me. He balled up his face and sniffed the air like he smelled something disgusting. "Did you fucking piss on yourself? Hell naw, shorty, it's time for you to get in the crib and stay there. Hurry and pass your phone. That car just crashed into a tree, and I need to call an ambulance instead of wasting time on your overdramatic self. There is a young girl down there who is really hurt."

Snatching the phone from my hand, he quickly punched in the numbers, not even offering me any help to get up or anything. "Yes, I would like to report a car accident at the corner of Henrietta Road and Finch Lane. Yes, the driver had made it out and she appeared to be dazed, but unharmed. She is sitting on the side of the road." He rattled off instructions to the 911 operator, all the while glaring at me like I did something wrong.

"Lox, I thought it was you. I would have died if something happened to you because of me. I fell trying to make my way to you. I thought they were going to kill you because you got me back as revenge. These people are sick. I didn't have a clue who I was messing with when I involved myself in that situation," I cried out.

"Sahnai, you are not that fucking special for someone to care where you are or try to knock me off behind your ass. And you were running to come do what? Save me? Your pitiful ass can't even save yourself. That situation I just got you out of was because of you. Don't look at me all surprised. I can't believe you thought you could run away after you created all this drama. Using men, stealing money and drugs. You were a real whore on the low."

I wondered what he heard. I wanted to explain, but he was already turning to go back to his car. "That's it, Lox? You don't even want to hear me out? Nothing? I was taken advantage of. He was my fathe—" Turning around faster than I'd ever seen anyone move, he grabbed me by the front of my yellow Bebe sweatsuit.

"Yo, B, nothing that you can say to me would change how I feel about your ass, trust me. I will have my mom call you to set up a time for you to see Q again," he said as he turned to walk away again.

Throwing myself down on the front steps, I cried and cried, yelling out to his retreating back through my tears. "Lennox, you don't even care about me one bit. After everything?"

With sad eyes, he turned to me one last time. "Sahnai, I care about you. You my baby moms, so I will always care about you, but I don't love you anymore."

With that, I watched him as he jogged over to help the injured passenger of the car that hit the tree that was right before his car. He waited with her until the ambulance came and her car was towed away. The whole time I wished I were by his side. He was a great guy, and I really fucked up with him. Hell, I had fucked up our great relationship before I ever met him. I sat outside with no shoes, socks, or jacket on, just shivering in the cold, watching him. I could see his muscular body as he stripped off his bloody shirt. It wasn't his blood, but the blood of the injured girl he saved. *Damn, I miss touching that body, kissing his chest, and moving lower.*

Realizing that the nasty, pissy smell was coming from me, I was so embarrassed. I hopped up from the stairs and opened the front door. Deciding I needed to relax, I grabbed a bottle of red wine, no glass, and walked upstairs to run a bubble bath. Pouring in some of the Sensual Collection cherry vanilla–scented bubble bath from Bath & Body Works, I turned the water to hot and grabbed a garbage bag from under the sink. Throwing the ruined sweatsuit inside, I tied a knot in the top and threw it outside the bathroom door. I thought about grabbing a book to read or playing some music but decided against it. I was just going to take some time in the quiet to think about my next move. *Do I even want to stay here? Maybe I should try a new city like Miami or*

L.A. There is nothing here for me anymore but my baby.
My grandmother barely speaks to me, and my cousin
hates me. I can't blame her. I really did her dirty.

A Month Later

I sat outside the park, watching Alani with my son, and my cousin, Inaya, was holding a baby in a front carrier, so I couldn't see the face. I could tell it was a girl from all the pink blankets wrapped around her. It was unseasonably warm for March, and I guessed they were out here taking advantage of the nice weather. I lost my man, my son, and the person who was like my sister to this plain little girl. I couldn't blame anyone but myself. I had been a fuckup my whole life, and I was just tired now. I should have been the one over there chilling with Aiden and Inaya. I had never even seen my cousin's baby, but thank God for her existence, because if I had not missed the baby shower, no one would have ever figured out I was missing.

That was how much I meant to my friends and family, and to Lox. I saw the messages they all left me on my phone, all the "fuck you's" and "you ain't shit for not seeing your son" messages. Hell, I could have died in a carbon-monoxide incident, and no one would have ever known or cared. That was me, a nobody, and I was invisible to everyone around me except when I did something to piss them off. I knew Q loved me in his own way, but I had been gone so long that when he visited me, his conversations were filled with talk about his daddy and mommy Alani. I couldn't be mad at him, not my sweet boy. He was innocent in this whole situation. Going home, I decided today would be the day. I couldn't handle this life another day. I closed my eyes and pictured Junior blowing his brains out looking at a picture of me.

Now it was my time to join my parents wherever they ended up. I believed in God, but I didn't think He was accepting any of us into His kingdom. I went home and took a shower using my favorite Victoria's Secret scent, Love Spell. I felt the hot water beat down on my skin and enjoyed my last shower. I got out and used the matching lotion, and then I combed my hair out and curled my bob to perfection. Putting on a pair of black tights and a white-and-black V-neck tee that said "Princess" in big letters, I looked in the mirror one last time. I didn't think there was a specific outfit you should wear to die so this would do. Sitting down with my favorite picture of me, Lox, li'l Q, and Aiden, I took a pen and paper and began writing my goodbyes.

> *To my dearest Lox,*
> *I saw a picture the other day at the museum. I followed Alani there after she took the kids to the park. This picture, well, painting really, was of a mother, father, and a little girl in the middle. The parents were holding her hand, and she was looking up with a smile that looked content. She looked secure standing in front of the train in the picture. I wish I were that child. I have never felt that sense of security. My life was never secure. It was never like the little girl in the picture. I spent my whole childhood waiting for parents who were not coming to save me. My mother was already dead, and I never knew. I am the girl who had sex with her father and her brother. I don't belong here anymore.*
> *I have been watching our son with you and Alani, and I know he is better off without me. My baggage would scar him for life, and he deserves better than that. All I ask is that you tell him how much I loved*

him and keep telling him. Don't tell him the bad stuff. I want his memory of me to be pure.

Lennox, I always loved you. I know I made mistake after mistake when it came to you, but you were the only man who ever won my heart, and I have never stopped loving you. I am truly sorry for ruining what you and Alani have because I was just being selfish. Goodbye, Lox. I will miss watching you sleep on your belly and the way you run your hands through your dreads when you're frustrated, and most of all, I will miss being in your arms, feeling safe and loved.

I was crying ending the letter to Lox, but it had to be written. I needed him to know how I felt and why. I knew I had to write something to my cousin. No matter what, she was the closest thing I had to a sister, and what I was about to do would hurt her. I was always hurting her, but at least this time I would get to say I was sorry.

Dear Inaya,

I am sorry if this will hurt you, and please know that even with all the things I have done to you, I loved you. I just didn't know how to show it because no one had ever shown it to me. I know you did, but by that time, I was already so damaged and angry deep inside, I took it for granted. I could not see past being jealous of you, and if I could turn back the hands of time, I would. Please help look out for li'l Q and give him good memories of his mommy. I am asking not for me, but for him. I want him to have the best chance at life that he can, and I don't want him being scarred by my actions. Last, little cousin, I want to tell you I am so happy you found Phantom, Alani, Azia, and even Lox. You have the

family you always craved and dreamed of. Hold on
to it and cherish it, because being lonely is no place
for anyone.
    Love always and forever,
    Sahnai

Going in the lockbox in the hallway, I got the gun
that Lox insisted I have for safety after the kidnapping.
I wondered one more time if this was the right thing
to do. *Maybe I should try to get some help. Maybe*
someone could get the nightmares to go away. Picking
up my phone, I called Lox. Maybe he could help me.
After calling twice, I realized he wasn't going to answer
me. Dialing Inaya's number, it was the same thing. It
rang and rang until her voicemail came on. She sounded
happy in the message. "It's Inaya, leave a message after
the beep." Hanging up before the beep, I decided to just
do what I had to. No one answering me proved what
I already knew: they were all better off with me gone.
Picking up the gun, I looked at the picture of the family I
used to have.

Chapter 14

Inaya

Deciding to take my Audi to New Jersey for Azia's birthday party, I asked Alani if she and Vivy wanted to ride with me and the kids, and she said yeah. There was no telling who Phantom would be dragging along with him, and I wasn't about to let my feelings where he was concerned ruin my good time or my sissy's special day. I was looking forward to having a drink and getting out of the Roc. I pulled up to Alani's place, and she came out along with one Gucci duffel bag and a matching garment bag.

"Pop the trunk, sis. Let's get this show on the road," she yelled in an excited voice.

"I see your child has abandoned you just like mine. Kadia asked to ride with Uncle Lox, and now I know why—so she could ride with Vivy. Those two are like twins, and I guess Lox gives out better snacks or some shit," I said in a joking tone. I was happy that my baby had cousins to hang out with and be happy with. I prayed that Vivy would never turn on her the way that Sahnai did me. Noticing Alani looking kinda sad, I wondered what had been going on with her lately. Lox wouldn't even let Vivy come home until a week ago, and she had been walking around here looking like she lost her best friend.

We made good time to Jersey, and the venue was gorgeous. There was a red-carpet theme with a lot of bling, just like something Azia would love. I sat at the table with the girls, stalking my baby daddy with my eyes. Watching Phantom with Tamia, I felt empty. That was the only word I could think of. I couldn't help but think of all the love that was held in my heart for him. This back-and-forth game was getting to be too much, and sometimes I felt like it wasn't all his fault. He had been respectful since he came back, and he had even begun to accept the whole Marvin thing. Fuck, all I really wanted him to do was go fuck up Marvin and force me to be back with him. I wanted Phantom to want me, fight for me like I was the love of his life. Instead, he seemed content with Tamia. He didn't put her down or call her names, and she never walked around looking beaten down by their relationship like I was.

Seeing Kadia cling to Phantom, I was happy he had come home. His kids needed him. I needed him too, but I couldn't tell him that now. Feeling the uncontrollable urge to use the bathroom, I put the baby in her car seat. "Alani, can you watch her? I gotta pee," I asked, almost running to the restroom after she began cooing at the baby.

Breastfeeding meant I had to drink a lot of water, and I was sick of it. I was peeing more now than when I was pregnant. Taking a moment to just sit and get my emotions in check, I could hear the main door opening, so I decided to wipe, flush, and get the heck out of there before I started breaking down in front of one of Azia's party guests. Washing my hands, I looked up in the mirror in time to see Phantom in the mirror watching my every move.

"What the hell are you doing in here? You do know this is a ladies' room and you are a man, right?" As he moved closer to me, I felt his hands on my hips. I searched my brain for more protests. "What about Tamia?" I spit out as I felt his lips touch my neck and move down the dip in my silk shirt. He never even looked up from what he was doing.

Slowly, he unbuttoned the tiny buttons, leaving a kiss one by one. I was praying he would not undo my bra. I had these damn nursing pads in, and I was not trying to hear him clown me or become distracted from the feeling I was having between my legs. It was a throbbing mixed with a steady drip of my juices. I was craving his touch like he was food and I was starving. Trying not to moan too loudly, I stood there leaning up against the sink as he put his hand under my skirt and gently fingered my nude silk panties.

As fast as lightning on a rainy day, he was on his knees in front of me with my black skirt puffed around his head. His lips were racing up the inside of my legs, leaving wet trails as he continued farther up toward my throbbing pussy. *What the fuck is happening? He has never done anything like this before.* If he was teasing me, I was going to take my box cutter and slash his ass, because I was ready to feel his lips on my clit. Finally, he spoke as he pulled my moist panties to the side. His breath was hot and blowing on my pearl. "Iny, you better not fall," he said with a smirk in his voice.

Finally—the moment I had craved for months, shit, for over a year when we first met. His tongue reached out, slow and uncertain. He timidly licked my clit. He pushed his finger inside of me, and I felt like I was going to die from pleasure. *What is happening?* The room was spinning, and my eyes began rolling in the back of my head. "Oh, my God, Phantom, you are trying to kill me. This shit feels so good. I can't hold back anymore. I need to cum," I explained as my body began to shake and my orgasm took over. I could feel my juices flow into his mouth, and he licked them up. I knew we were not finished when he dropped his jeans and pulled out his monster. *Shit, it's been so long. I wonder if I can handle it, but I'm sure going to try. I miss this dick. This dick belongs to me. While I have the chance, I am going to fuck him so good he won't even remember Tamia exists.*

Bending over the sink and pulling up my skirt, I invited him to come to his pussy. When I felt him slide in, I gasped in shock at how he filled me, how he made every nerve in my body come to life with each stroke. He bent down and began whispering in my ear, "Inaya, this is my pussy. I will kill Marvin or any other man who ever comes close to my pussy. I need you, and I am sorry for everything I have put you through. I am going to prove to you that I love you." When he uttered the words "I love you," he began fucking me hard, and I made sure to tighten my pussy and throw it back. Before I knew it, someone was knocking at the main door that he somehow locked, and he was unloading his thick cum deep inside my belly. *Fuck, I am not even on birth control.*

Hearing the door handle shake again, I hurried and ran some water and wiped up as best I could with wet paper towels.

"Yo, chill the fuck out. We're gonna be out in a second," Phantom yelled at whoever was at the door.

I could hear someone say in a shocked voice, "Was that a man?" and then a few ladies were laughing. Fumbling around with the final button, I decided I would fix it at the table, and I hurried to unlock the door before the wrong people found us in there. I walked out with Phantom right behind me. A few of Azia's friends were standing there with looks of envy and awe in their eyes. I was sure they wished they were the ones in the bathroom having Phantom fuck their brains out, but too fucking bad for them, because it was me.

I walked to the table slowly. Shit, slow was all I could do because my pussy was beat the fuck up and my legs were rubber from the back-to-back orgasms he gave me. As soon as I sat down at the table, I tried to discreetly button the last button on my shirt, only to hear Alani and Azia laughing at me and giving me looks like they knew what I'd been up to.

Trying to keep my voice low, I leaned over closer to the girls. "I know you both know what the fuck I did. Just shut up about it, please. I cannot even go into it here, or I will be an emotional wreck. Plus, y'all asses not about to be clowning me for indulging in bathroom sex." Seeing that Kahnia was awake and cooing in her baby seat, I decided to bring her to her daddy's table so he could spend some time with her. I knew how he missed his kids when he had to be out of town or in the streets.

Walking over, kissing on my baby's face, I wasn't paying attention to the angry look on Tamia's face and the amused one on Phantom's. "Phantom, where the fuck were you, and what the hell is this white shit on your jeans?" she questioned him ferociously.

Trying not to laugh out loud, I began to choke when this nigga responded, "Babe, that's frosting, and I was in the bathroom shitting. Anything else you want or need to know? You must want to know what color the shit was." This nigga had the nerve to be openly laughing at her, and she began shaking her head okay. The frosting on the cake was chocolate, not vanilla, so if she wanted to live in denial, more power to her. Finally looking away from my cum that had gotten all over Phantom's Diesel jeans, she noticed me standing there.

"Can we help you? You're always here. Every time I turn around, you're there, so what the fuck do you want now?" she said in a rude tone.

"Bitch, damn right I am always here. I will always be here, right next to him. I am here to bring our daughter to visit her father. I hope you won't be such a pain in the ass when we have our next child," I shot out there as I handed a smiling Phantom his baby and turned to walk back to my seat. Not being able to help this feistiness that came over me, I mumbled to myself, "Tired of fucking with these professional side bitches. I wonder if we pay her unemployment when she gets fired."

Phantom

Well, shit, I guess all I had to do a long time ago was lick Inaya's pussy and fuck the shit out of her ass, and she would have gotten a backbone faster. I looked at Tamia's mouth move with complaints that were silent to me since I tuned her out after I had some fun telling her that another woman's pussy juices was vanilla frosting. Nodding my head and making faces at the baby, hoping she would laugh, was my only focus. I was beginning to regret bringing Tamia's whiny ass at all. All she was doing was blocking me trying to get my girl back. I really didn't even ask her to come. She kind of invited herself along. I didn't fight it because last week I saw that Inaya went on a date with Marvin's ol' bitch ass. I didn't say shit, even though I wanted to kill that nigga just thinking about the two of them.

It was a Friday, and I came to the house just to see what my kids were up to. I was surprised as hell to see Alani lounging on the couch and Inaya walking down the stairs wearing a tight-ass black dress that had the back out. I was mad as hell when she calmly told me she was going to dinner with Marvin because he missed her since he had not seen her since before the baby. All I was thinking was, *so the fuck what?* and how much I wanted to stay and fuck her ass to sleep. I left when she did, but I made sure I came back in an hour and sent Alani home. I watched the kids and waited to see what time Inaya brought her ass back in the house. I was ready to fight if she came in looking like she fucked or smelling like she fucked. Instead, she came home before Kadia was even asleep, with a bag of leftovers from Black & Blue.

Feeling someone hitting me on the arm, I looked up to see Tamia's angry face as I snapped out of my memory. "What the fuck you putting yo' hands on me for? It's like you don't know I fuck up females too," I told her, all while cutting my eyes her way.

"Babe, I am ready to go back to the hotel. I am so tired. Maybe I am pregnant. We should try for a baby soon so you can have kids with the woman you're actually with instead of some pop off."

Feeling anger rush to my head, I almost fell out of my seat. I had to remember I had baby girl in front of me. *Did this fucking dummy call Inaya a pop off when she was the pop off?*

"Yo, B, it's time for you to go. This is your first and last friendly warning. I am never having kids with anyone but Inaya, and if you ever feel the urge to call her a name or disrespect her in any way, then you'd better think again. Don't even let that shit cross your mind. I will see it in your eyes. Now get you an Uber and wait out in the hallway or something, because you just pissed me all the way off." I got up and grabbed the baby off the table to walk over to where Lox was.

"Nigga, you look like you trying so hard not to kill ol' girl. What the fuck she do, and why you got white shit all over your pants?"

Looking at my cousin with a "fuck you" face, I laughed at his last comment. *Damn, is the shit on my pants*

*making it that obvious that I was around here fucking
something? Something sweet if you ask me.*

"Son, this bitch is annoying as hell. She called Inaya
a pop off and started talking about she thinks she's
pregnant and she hopes she is so we can be together. I
didn't even entertain that pregnant shit, and I almost
bashed her head in for calling Inaya a pop off. Anyway, I
told her it was time to go and sent her on her way. I am
proud of myself for not showing out, mainly because
my little shorties are here and I am trying to be a better
person for them."

Running his hands through his dreads, he shook his
head, laughing. "She's lucky I ain't hear what she said
about my li'l sis. The funny part is how long you and Iny
were in the bathroom earlier. Looks like you tryin'a get
another baby with someone, but it's not your girl."

I couldn't even look at him without laughing, so I just
smirked and looked around the room to make sure the
party was going well. The girls were on the dance floor
moving their bodies like none of them had a man at home.
Shit, due to my and my cousin's nonsense, none of them
did. I hoped this shit changed for both of us sometime
soon. This love business was really something else, and
I never thought I would be going through it. "Lox, you
need to take Alani's ass in the bathroom and do like me,
son, before it's too late." I pointed in the direction I was
looking. Some nigga came up to Alani and was talking all
in her ear.

Taking the baby to the table with Miss Wanda and
Nadia, I decided to go follow Lox, who was about to
create a scene.

"Yo, nigga, you can keep it pushing because this one
right here is already spoken for. Alani, I don't know why
you fucking playing, ma. You for real standing in front of
me letting some punk-ass nigga talk to you?" Lox went

off as soon as he made it over there. I guessed I wasn't needed, because as soon as his wild ass pulled up his shirt and showed ol' boy his Glock, he ran for the door. Now he just had to deal with Alani, who snatched her arm away from him and stormed to the other side of the room. All the while, she, Azia, and Inaya were looking back at us like they would fuck us up if they could. *Oh, well, they will get over it. This is a no-flex zone over here, and these niggas better get the point and fast.*

Waking up at Inaya's house, I knew today was the day I was breaking things off with Tamia. I thought she knew this day was coming. Shit, if not, then she was stupid. I would have loved to say I felt bad, or sad, some emotion in my heart, but I didn't. I didn't even trust her ass after I found out she knew Cudjie. When it came to this nigga being involved with anyone or anything close to me, it always brought bullshit my way. Since the baby had been born, I had become more aggressive with the search for this nigga so I could eliminate this problem for good. I needed to make sure my family was safe.

My phone began ringing, and the number I had saved under bitch nigga flashed across my screen. Pressing reject, I went back to watching some mob documentary on TV, and it rang again. For the past few months my pops had been trying to call me here and there, and now he was blowing me up. Putting him on the block list, I jumped up, hearing a knock at the door.

Checking the camera and seeing it was Lox, I let this nigga in so we could talk about some of this shit that was going on. "Son, I know these niggas think I am slipping, but I am not. I have even had someone trailing Shawnie's ass for a while now. The funny thing about that is what I found out about her. Another situation that, of course, led back to my baby brother. Like, will this nigga ever not be a thorn in my fucking side? When we were in Jersey the other day, I stopped through the old hood in Brooklyn and saw some of our boys. Me and Jeremey were kicking it, and he was telling me about his new baby and shit, and I was telling him I had two daughters and all that good shit. So this nigga looks at me and says, 'What about your son?' Nigga, when I tell you, I thought this dude was smoking dope."

Lox began trying to figure this shit out before I even finished telling him the whole story, ol' impatient-ass nigga. "So, wait, what son? Which one of those bitches from back in the day is walking around with your li'l man? I told you to stop being so wild back in the day. You were fucking anything that moved."

Cutting him off by putting up my hand, I sat back in my chair and was happy as hell Inaya was not home to hear this bullshit. I thought I really needed my own little spot, because I was always here or at Azia's house. Shit, somewhere private. "No, my dude, I ain't got a son unless his ass cooking in Inaya's belly right now. This nigga told me Shawnie has a three-year-old son who looks like me, so he thought it was my kid. Now I go check with the lookout, and he sends me pictures of the kid. As soon as I saw this little nigga, I realized I had seen him before at my mom and pop's crib when I went over there looking for this nigga Cudjie."

"Hell no, Shawnie was fucking your brother? These bitches have no loyalty or self-respect. Well, one thing I can say is you dodged a bullet with that bitch, and so did I with Alani's scandalous ass. Son, did I even tell you that bitch cheated on Travis, and Vivy is from some wack-ass dude named Ray?"

Interrupting my cousin, I couldn't believe what he was saying to me. "My nigga, that little bighead nigga Ray from the west side is Vivy's pops?"

"Man, he ain't shit no more, so I guess we will never know. He was threatening Alani and shit, so I got rid of his ass. Vivy got me. She doesn't need no other daddy in her life. Fuck him. He knew who Alani was with, and he still wanted to come for her."

I just sat shaking my head, listening to my cousin continue talking shit. "On some real shit, son, we gotta get rid of your brother. He is a fucking pain in my ass. I think he had something to do with the spot getting hit on Dewey the other day. You know I am not about losing any fucking money, and that nigga Phine been moving funny, too, so we may have to get rid of him next. He has never gotten over that shit with Sahnai. Hell, I told him the other day I was gonna fuck him up for looking at me like I was some bitch. I also told him he could have her ol' worn-out, scandalous ass. She needed someone in her corner, and it would never be me again."

"Yo, that shit with Sahnai fucked me up. I was truly stuck because the way she broke my girl's heart had me wanting to kill her ass, but at the same time, she is Q's mom, and I understand how hard it is to have mom issues, and I didn't want to be the one to give him those problems. I just know you better not start fucking with her ass again, or she's gonna be getting a permanent home in the dirt somewhere," I promised my cousin. That bitch would not be coming back into our lives, fucking up shit for him or my wifey. After me and my cousin made plans to go and get this fuck nigga Cudjie and decided to keep a closer eye on Phine, he left, and I lay around the house, waiting until the evening when I could meet up with Tamia and cut her ass off.

Chapter 15

Lox

I woke up today and felt lost. There was no other word for it. I always tried to be a good person. I dealt with my workers fairly, and some of these young niggas were plotting on me. I treated Sahnai like a queen, but she played games and broke my heart. I still looked out for her, because real love just doesn't fade away like some people make it seem. I forgave her for everything, I just never told her. Now I would never get to tell her or make amends with her. She was so damaged, so hurt, ever since she was a small child. Looking at the letter she left me one more time, I couldn't begin to understand the pain she had lived with. How alone she felt. How disgusted she was with herself for shit that wasn't even her fault. But see, a nigga like me was just being a nigga, and when I found out she fucked her daddy and her brother, I made her feel ashamed and nasty. I made her feel worse than she already did. I mean, shit, it wasn't like she knew.

I never thought about how depressed she looked when I stopped by or how sad she looked when I took Q back home with me. I didn't even give her a chance to be a mom again. Hell, she had him the first couple of years, and he turned out great. He was healthy, clean, and fed well. Now he would not even remember his mother when he grew up. Speaking of Q, here he came to check on me. I could hear his footsteps racing down the hall.

"Daddy, what are you doing? Daddy, come play," he demanded, grabbing my hands and pulling me toward the playroom. I wanted to let the tears fall looking at him and how much he looked like Sahnai, but I didn't want him to know I was sad, so I put a smile on my face and made my way into the war zone of toys.

"Lox, are you in here?" I heard Alani calling me from the front of the house.

"Lox, I missed you so much. I want to come home and not leave anymore!" yelled Vivy as she ran to me and jumped in my arms.

"Aww, Vivy, you would miss Mommy, so you have to go home and keep her company sometimes. Why don't you and Q play in here so I can go and talk to Mommy?" I offered her as a compromise. She shook her head and turned the TV on to some cartoon about a little girl and a bear. Looked like *Little Red Riding Hood* or some shit. I grabbed a sleeping Aiden from Alani, and he began to cry in his sleep for his mommy.

"Don't be snatching him from me. He is good," she said as she took him back and gently rocked him from side to side.

"Man, his ass gonna be too spoiled. He is good with his medicine, so he can let me have some time with his mommy. Lay him down in his crib or something. I need to talk to you." I said that I wanted to talk, but as she went to lay the baby down, I didn't know what I wanted to do. I worked like a fucking dog to get this girl back, only for her to not turn out to be who I thought she was. Seeing Alani walk out of the bedroom, I grabbed her arm and led her to my room. Closing the door, I pulled her closer to me.

"Lox, what are you doing? The kids are still up downstairs, and you know they will burst in here at any moment."

Not caring about what she was saying, I locked the door and led her to the bed. I removed her white and blue T-shirt to see her breasts spring free. Damn, she was walking around with no bra on. *What the fuck!* Maybe she was on her way to fuck another nigga.

I sucked on her nipples, and she began dry humping me as I laid my body on hers. I could feel the wetness through her panties and sweatpants. I missed this pussy so much. It didn't compare to anything I had been getting in the streets. Pulling her pants down roughly, I stripped out of my clothes and picked her up so I could move her to the top of the bed.

"Alani, I want to fuck you. You want this dick, baby?" I asked her while playing with her wet pussy. Her moaning and winding on my fingers let me know she felt the same. Pushing her legs up to her ears, I sank in her pussy balls deep.

"Arghhh!" she screamed, feeling all of me. Not stopping, I pulled out and went in deep again. I could feel her juices getting all over the bed and splashing me.

Turning her over, I felt my dick get harder when she spread her legs and arched her back. She began fingering herself while I sat back and watched. Shit, I couldn't hold out anymore. I moved her finger out of the way and replaced it with my cock. Letting her bounce up and down on my dick, I couldn't hold back anymore. Her pussy was too tight and too wet. "Fuck, girl, what are you doing to me? Cum with me, Lani. Don't hold back." I pulled her hair and felt her pussy squeeze my dick. That was all it took. My nut filled her insides, and I collapsed on the bed next to her. I knew the kids would be fine since Miss Wanda was downstairs in the kitchen.

Listening to the kids run around in the hallway while getting ready for bed, I smiled to myself. Alani stretched next to me in her sleep and then curled deeper in my arms. I thought I would be able to sleep after that bomb-ass sex, but nope, sleep still wouldn't come. I didn't think I had been able to sleep since I found Sahnai at her kitchen table with her brains splattered all over the lace curtains and white walls. It was even on the orange placemats in front of her. Then there was the picture of me, her, and the boys at a beach. It was one of the family pictures we took in the short time we were all together as a family. The blood and brain matter hit the frame so hard it broke the glass right in the middle of the frame. This image haunted me every time I closed my eyes. This wasn't some nigga who stole from me, or some nigga in the streets. This was the girl I spent years loving, missing, and looking for.

And how did I explain to our son someday when he was grown up that his mother was so injured inside that she killed herself? I could still see the look on Inaya's face when she found out we couldn't even have a funeral. I asked her if she wanted the ashes, and she just shook her head and said they belonged with me, with her son. So much had been going on. I had not spoken to my father in months, not since I confronted him about cheating on my mother and she decided to defend him. I washed my hands of the situation. Hell, if she liked it, I loved it. I guessed no one was there to raise her to have any self-re-spect, and I was tired of fighting to change people, to help people. Hell, they just ended up doing what they wanted in the end anyway, so fuck it. She could stay home, sad, and he could fuck everyone in the U.S. and Jamaica—the whole world for all I cared.

I had been thinking about leaving this place, just tak-ing the boys and going to Florida or Atlanta, somewhere with no snow and no memories of Sahnai haunting me. I only reconsidered when I considered Vivy and Alani. I couldn't leave them. I wished she were still mine.

I would have bred her ass, and once she had my baby, we could have all moved together. I didn't know how to deal with her anymore. I still loved her, but the shit she told me about her cheating on Travis had me fucked up in the head. I wanted to love her and be with her, but now I couldn't trust her. It was like I was turning into Phantom.

I wanted a new life. *This drug game ain't for me anymore. I know Phantom is going to be mad because his life is different from mine. He lives for the score, the kill, anything that gets his heart racing and his adrenaline pumping. He has always been like that.* I remembered that he would steal from the corner store just because he enjoyed the chase as a child. He skipped classes sometimes just to see if he could get away with it.

I had to figure out a way to live if I was going to get serious about leaving this lifestyle alone. Maybe I could open a hotel or buy a nanny agency. I knew those places made bread because I paid my nanny a ton of fucking money to help with the kids. I guessed I should see a financial advisor first. I couldn't jump out of the game tomorrow, but I could start making a plan. I wouldn't be retiring as some millionaire, maybe a thousand-aire, if that was a thing. I could just hear all the shit Phantom would be talking now, but a nigga was so tired. I mean, tired deep inside. I wouldn't be giving a fuck.

The next day, Alani left without saying a word to me. I thought she knew my feelings for her were all messed up since her confession, and I was sure that had her emotional. Sex always seemed to make women emotional. I mean, I would never turn my back on her or intentionally hurt her, especially now. I would never do that again, but I had just been burned by too many women . . . shit, too many people. Since the kids were at school and Wanda took Aiden to some Gymboree class, I was in this big-ass house all alone. Deciding on Hennessy for breakfast, I poured a glass straight and went to sit in the living room. As soon as my ass hit the couch, someone was ringing the doorbell. Checking the cameras, I noticed Inaya standing outside, looking impatient. Snatching open the door before she and the baby froze to death, I looked at her with a concerned face.

"Iny, is everything okay?" I asked.

"Well, first of all, it took forever for you to answer. I think I need a key so I don't have to wait from now on. You know how much this little girl weighs? Like ten pounds, and the baby seat is like thirty," she mouthed off. I couldn't help but smile as I grabbed the baby from her. Inaya really found her voice, and since she had, she had not shut up. Grabbing the baby and taking her little pink snowsuit off of her, I made silly faces as she reached out and grabbed my nose.

"Iny, what's up? You need money or something? You and Phantom beefing again?" I asked, trying to feel out her reason for this visit. She shook her head in what looked like a disgusted manner, and I was confused. I couldn't think of any reason for Inaya to be mad at me, so it had to be my cousin. *Here we go again.* Hell, the other day he told me he was going to work shit out with li'l sis, but it looked like he was taking his sweet time. Marvin was going to snatch her away if he didn't hurry up.

"Lox, I am here because of you. We need to talk about a few things. The first thing is I need you to stop blaming yourself for my cousin's death. Sahnai was my cousin, just like my sister, and let me tell you something. Even in death, she was selfish. I have loved Sahnai for as long as I could remember. I looked up to her and watched her every move. That is why I know she was selfish. I remember how she would put me down and lie and get me in trouble just because. I knew her flaws, but I didn't care because we were family. I know you loved her and that you did everything you could to save her, but she didn't want to be saved. She didn't care about me or you or Q when she killed herself. She cared about making you feel bad for not being with her, even after all of her bullshit. I wish my cousin were still here. I wish I'd checked on her and looked in on her or answered her call the day she died." Inaya stopped there because she was having trouble speaking through her tears. I knew she was hurting as much as me, if not more.

"Okay, li'l sis, hush, don't cry. I will do my best to let go of the guilt and some of the pain, for you and for li'l Q. Now what was the other thing you wanted to talk about?" I asked her while giving her a side hug since I was still holding the baby.

Wiping the tears from her eyes and sniffling a little, Inaya got herself together before she spoke. "I want to talk to you about Alani. Now don't say shit. Just sit back and listen. I am watching you hurt my friend, someone who is like a sister to me, and hurt yourself, my favorite big brother. All because of what? Because Alani cheated on her fucked-up ex-boyfriend years ago? Alani sat home in a loveless relationship every day. She was subjected to constant disrespect from other women, and after getting jumped by one of Travis's many girlfriends and then him, she decided she was done. She went out and got drunk and saw a guy she knew from around the way. Next thing you know, one thing led to another, and they slept together one time.

"It's not great, but it happened. It has nothing to do with you and her. She loves you with her whole soul, so do not fuck this up. You're sitting over here telling yourself you don't trust Alani, but that is a damn lie. You trust her with something more important than your heart. You trust her with your children. She still has a key to your home where you lay your head. So stop the foolishness and go get your girl! Now what do you have to eat in here? I am starving." She ended with a serious-ass look on her face as she jumped up and went to my kitchen to find food.

"Umm, Inaya, why you so damn hungry? Let me find out you pregnant again," I shouted at her from the other room. I really wanted to ask her when she became so bossy and so smart, and how I was supposed to fix this mess I had created with Alani.

Alani

I have tried all I could to reach Lox. The devil on my shoulder kept telling me to say fuck him, to be mad that he was grieving for his baby mom, but I couldn't. I knew what it was like to lose the first person you ever fell in love with and to find out that they were not the person you thought they were when they were alive. Looking down at the sleeves of my red sweater, I pulled at the ends. It was a habit I had when I was stressed out, and I was definitely stressed right now. I never wished this on Sahnai or on li'l Q. Now there was another child we had to raise and help figure out why this cruel world snatched their parent away. I felt guilty. If I had not entered the picture, maybe Sahnai and Lox would have worked shit out and she would still be alive. All of this hurt and pain, and he and I didn't even end up together.

Walking down the hall to Aiden's room, I poked my head in to see him sleeping peacefully in his crib. He was sleeping on his stomach with his butt in the air. He was with me more than ever now. He basically lived with me. Even on nights like tonight when Vivy was with Lox and Q, Aiden would stay with me. I loved him so much. I didn't even care that he wasn't Lox's child by blood. That didn't make a difference. He was our child. He didn't have anyone else, and I would never turn my back on him. I was walking kind of slow still from the beating my pussy got at Lox's house yesterday. I didn't even stay the full night after that. Even though he was there holding me, I could tell he was distant. I guessed he just couldn't get over the fact that I cheated on Travis and that I didn't know who Vivian's father was. I was young and dumb, and I honestly had no excuse for what I did. I was just human. I would never throw in his face the fact that he had cheated on every girl he ever had, including me. I didn't even have the heart to argue. Look at what the lies and secrets got me. I could have lost my life or gotten my child hurt the way crazy-ass Ray was acting.

Jumping on my bed, I turned the TV on to keep me company and pulled my pillow closer. I was hugging that thing like it was my only friend. Seeing that *Twilight* was on, I tortured my already-tearful heart and decided to watch it. *Fuck, this little pale chick got two niggas fighting over her. I know I would have chosen the wolf dude because his body is on ten.*

Waking up to feel someone else's presence, I reached next to my bed for my Taser.

"Damn, ma, that's how you gonna do your man and shit?" Lox joked as he climbed into the bed next to me. I could feel the tears start before I could stop them. "Ma, I've been stupid. You had a past like I had a past, and I am so sorry I treated you like shit. You've been my rock and have been by my side through all of the bullshit in my life, and I love you, ma."

Chapter 16

Phantom

Looking at the kids as they walked with Nadia to Lox's house, I felt like my heart was finally able to beat. Finally, I had my family back, finally I had a family of my own, but for some reason, I still didn't feel right. Growing up in the ghetto, living a life of crime and murder, I knew when something was not right, and something was not right. I felt like I just got back some sense of control over stuff, over my life and my family. Now I felt like things were unraveling again. I was still not convinced that Phine and Tamia were who they said they were. Something with her was not adding up, and this shit with Phine obsessing over Sahnai and her death was rubbing me the wrong way. Did he think we killed her ass?

I moved to the house with Inaya and my kids, and I was finally able to show shawty I could be the man she needed. I was having no problems keeping my dick to myself these days because I had a lot to lose. Iny may not have been a real rah-rah hood bitch who would go fuck up every ho who looked my way, but seeing the look of pain I used to cause her on her face was like someone taking my breath away. I wouldn't fight loving her another moment because life was too short to make those kinds of mistakes. At first I questioned her about that nigga Marvin, only to find out she ended their friendship the night she went on that dinner date. The old me would have called her a liar or something worse, but the man who loved Inaya knew she was being honest. Looking down at my phone, I saw Tamia's ass was still trying with the whole "I am in love with you" shit. *I may have to change my phone number.* All of that would have to wait though, because today I was taking my girl out on a date. Just me and her, no kids and no family. She deserved all of my attention.

"Ma, you ready?" I asked, walking into the bedroom. She looked ready to me—ready for me to bend her over and fuck her in that tiny-ass white and mint green striped dress she had on. It fit her like a glove and had a slit up the side. Spring was just creeping in, so she paired it with a form-fitting white blazer and nude heels. *Inaya better not get too used to those little-ass dresses and heels because I know her ass is pregnant again.* Last night she was eating hot popcorn dipped in honey mustard. Her cravings gave her away. Making my way to open the door of her new white Porsche Panamera, I helped her in the passenger seat. I drove so she could relax a few minutes and not have to do anything. She had her hands full with the baby and Kadia all day. Those two girls were spoiled, and I had been away a lot more, handling business in Miami and Texas. You know this nigga was not ever leaving the game. I loved this shit.

As soon as we pulled up to Black & Blue, I parked and walked around to help her out of the car. If I could tell Inaya was pregnant again, I wondered why she hadn't told me yet. As soon as she walked in the door, I felt something like fire hit me in my chest. *What the fuck!* I looked down and saw blood leaking through my white button-up shirt. It took me a full five seconds to realize I was shot. Pushing Inaya inside, all I could hear was her screaming my name. I couldn't stop to see what was going on with her because I needed to focus on killing whoever was trying to kill me. I grabbed my nine off my waist and began firing in the direction I thought the bullets were coming from. I ran from the doorway with my side on fire because I wanted the gunfire away from my shawty.

Rounding the corner, I saw a figure hiding behind a trash can. As soon as I got closer with my gun out, I realized it was my punk-ass father. "Nigga, I always knew you wanted me dead. I can't believe you would kill your oldest son!" I yelled. So this was why he kept calling me and trying to get information on my life. I guessed he thought I was going to invite him into my family's life so he could get rid of me easier. As he stood up, I noticed Cudjie's lifeless body lying next to him. *What the hell is going on?*

"Son, let me explain. It is not me trying to kill you. All along, it was your brother and your mother who had been trying to get rid of you and plotting on the pretty girl you have kids with. I found out he was coming to kill you, and I came to stop him. You don't understand the pain I have to live with knowing that I created someone so evil."

For some reason, I believed him. He looked old, way older than the last time I saw him, and hollow, like the life had been sucked out of him. Deciding I wasn't sticking around to comfort his punk ass, I ran back to the front. I had to make sure my future wife was good. "Ma, you a'ight?" I yelled, running up to her and holding her close. She looked pale and scared. Her arms were holding me so tight I could barely breathe.

"Phantom, you're hurt. Baby, don't leave me. Don't leave us," she cried and placed my hand on her belly. I guessed she knew about the baby after all. Feeling her hot tears, I could hear the sirens, but everything was getting dark all around me. The last thing I remembered thinking about was the ring I had in my pocket for Inaya, before everything went black.

Inaya

One Year Later

Waking up this morning alone in the bed, I felt the sunshine on my face. It made me smile because now I could sleep in the dark. Now seeing the sunshine through the window meant a new day with my family, the family I always wanted but didn't think I deserved. I knew that our life was not perfect. There was no fairy tale here, and I was not Cinderella. Even after being shot three times by his brother, Phantom told me straight up he was never leaving the streets alone, and I didn't ask him to. And even though he learned to respect me more, Phantom was just Phantom, and his attitude was still rude as fuck. There were days I had to really find my new bad-ass Inaya and go head-to-head with him. But not today. Today I was marrying the love of my life, and he was who he was, but I loved him.

Looking at the bag from David's Bridal hanging from the closet door, I could feel the butterflies in my stomach. I smoothed my hand over my flat belly. Thank God for that, because Phantom's ass seemed to have a plan to keep me pregnant. So much had changed in a year. We had a son two months ago named Jahdair Jr., and I was not interested in any more kids, but he had an idea that I was having one more. Hell no. I graduated with my bachelor's and still had not started my career, but as soon as Junior hit preschool, I was going to be in someone's classroom teaching.

Lox and Alani were back together but moving really slowly in their relationship. I was trying to get them to do a double wedding, but they both said they were not ready. Alani needed to have another baby because I was tired of being the only one around here with a big belly. Lox had been washing his dirty money and opening several legit businesses because he was ready to leave the streets alone. I was truly happy for my sis and brother for making things work. I mean, the situation was not the best, but love won in the end.

I could never have imagined that I could have a happy ending. The day Phantom was shot outside of the restaurant, I thought I had lost him. I prayed over him for weeks while he got better. I knew he was annoyed with me hovering over him so much. They found his mother strangled to death, and his father turned himself in for her murder. All along, his mother was truly pulling the strings on a lot of evil shit. I wouldn't be surprised if she was the reason his father stayed away when he was a kid. I was hoping that, one day, Phantom would get some counseling to help him deal with all that he had been through, but knowing him, he wouldn't go.

Azia finally started dating someone, this guy named Jrock who worked with Phantom and Lox. He was a little creepy to me, always watching people, and he barely spoke, but if little sis was happy, then so was I. He did seem to smile when he saw Azia, and the kids all liked him. Thank God Jrock was able to handle her spending habits, because she had not slowed down on the shopping one bit. She made me buy three dresses for this day alone.

Before it was time to go, I took a few more minutes to reflect on my life. I became sad thinking about Sahnai. She should have been here today, fixing my hair and clipping in my veil, telling me that I was making the right choice or that she was proud of me. I knew she was not the best cousin to me, but she was all I ever had. We made it through hell growing up, and now she was gone. Looking up at the clouds, I whispered, "Sahnai, I love you, and I know you are here in spirit." Taking one last look at myself in the mirror, I walked out the door to go and meet my destiny.

The End

Also Available

If I Was Your Girlfriend:

An Atlanta Tale

A Romance Novel by

Marlon McCaulsky

Nobody's perfect, but you're perfect for me

Chapter One

Ladies' Night

RASHIDA

"I tell all my hoes, 'Rake it up, break it down, bag it up.' Fuck it up, fuck it up. Back it up, back it up," Taylor rapped at the top of her lungs while two-stepping to the beat.

I once heard someone say that you were defined by who your friends were; and if that was true, I was in good company. Most of the time. Taylor Fenty, Joyce Roland, and Denise Varner were my closest friends. We'd been close since our teen days at Decatur High School, and now as grown twentysomething women, we had the type of bond that made us more like sisters than anything else.

Taylor had decided to go all out for her twenty-sixth birthday, so of course, we had to be there, and by there, I meant at the sexiest strip club in Atlanta. As soon as we stepped through the doors, the aroma of buffalo wings filled our nostrils. Going farther inside, past security, we were greeted by a voluptuous hostess who had more curves than Jessica Rabbit on steroids. She gave us a wide smile, and I gave her the name of the birthday girl.

She escorted us to our reserved section near the stage. As we weaved through the crowded club, the dimly lit pink and blue fluorescent lights illuminated the way. The demographics of folks in here ranged from couples on dates to men who looked like they worked at JPMorgan Chase and everything in between. An assortment of liquors was being served, and half-naked women were onstage, bouncing to a ratchet beat. Hell, I was bopping to the music too. I had heard that a former stripper named Jasmine now ran the club, and she had transformed it from a hole-in-the-wall to an upscale establishment. Looked like the rumors were true.

"What the hell is this?" Joyce groused.

I didn't think Joyce was too happy after we got there. She was more bougie than hood. Not a snob in a bad way, but she carried herself in a way that some might find stuck up. If we got a few drinks in her, however, she would turn up. She was, in my opinion, an around-the-way beauty. She had the kind of body the brothers loved to watch—slim but thick in all the right places. The mustard-colored dress she wore had open shoulders and highlighted her round backside. Before we'd left my place, I'd done her hair in a sexy crinkle style, but the most alluring thing about Joyce was her pretty brown eyes.

"It's the Pink Palace. Don't act like you never been in a strip club before," Taylor replied. She was a natural-born party girl and was determined to have fun tonight. It was in her nature. She was of mixed heritage, half-Trinidadian, thanks to her father, and Irish on her mother's side, which gave her a caramel complexion. She was the shortest of us, at five feet two. Her bubbly personality and the way she seemed to be the center of attention always made people think she was famous. Tonight she was dressed in a tight gold spaghetti-strap dress that showed off her sexy curves. Her ample cleavage made it hard for men to keep their eyes on her beautiful face.

Earlier in the week, she had decided to dye her long naturally black hair an auburn shade. We called her the turnup queen, so naturally she had wanted to go to a strip club for her birthday.

Joyce frowned as she stared at the topless women dancing on the main stage. "Yes, I've been to a strip club before," she said sarcastically, "but I thought it was, like, a male revue going on tonight."

"Ah . . . no." Taylor smirked. "What fun would that be?"

Joyce glared at her, then looked at me. "'Shida, you knew too?"

"Yeah. It's not a big deal. Come on, Joyce, lighten up."

"I don't wanna sit here with some ho shaking her stank ass in my face."

Taylor stared at Joyce and shook her head. "Joyce, just relax. I just wanna see how it is in here. We don't have to stay long."

Joyce looked at me again, and I smiled. I looked at Denise, who looked like she was in a state of shock. This wasn't her thing at all. I knew for sure she was uncomfortable. She considered herself a plain-Jane type of girl, even though she could be as sexy as any woman dancing in this club. Denise was slim and beautiful, at an even five feet four, with a body that would make men drool. She had a figure that was built for high fashion and runways, but she was way too modest to show it off in public. Tonight she wore a silver dress, with a black shawl draped over her shoulders. Her long black hair framed her beautiful face.

I stared at her. "Are you okay, Denise?"

"Ah . . . yeah. I'm fine."

I could tell by the look on her face she was anything but.

Joyce was just complaining for the sake of it, but Denise wasn't the party type at all. If it weren't for us,

Denise would have spent her whole college experience in her dorm, with a book in her face.

"If you're not feeling it, we can go," I told her.

Denise looked over my shoulder, and I knew Taylor was behind me, mean muggin' her. Denise forced a smile onto her face. "I'm okay. It's Taylor's b-day. Let's just do what she wants tonight."

Taylor smirked. "Well, if Wallflower can stay, so can you, Joyce."

Joyce exhaled. "All right, but I don't want them hoes touching me."

Denise rolled her eyes. I hated when Taylor threw shade at Denise. I would normally pull Taylor to the side and tell her to chill, but I decided not to scold her, since it was her birthday. That was the role I, an Afrocentric Jamaican girl, usually played in the group—the unofficial surrogate mother of us all.

My mother was from St. Catherine, Jamaica, and my father was born and raised in Birmingham, England. They met while my mother was attending university in England. A few years later they married and moved to Atlanta, Georgia, because my father had taken an executive position at PricewaterhouseCoopers. A few years after that, they had me and my little brother, Raheem. I inherited my mother's sense of style and my father's business sense, two things I cherished about them after their untimely death.

Tonight it was my mother's style I was channeling. I had recently unbraided my coiled locks, and they hung loose past my shoulders. I loved my natural hair. It made me feel free and sexy. It wasn't always easy to maintain, but it was all me, all natural. I wore tan thigh-high boots with a black and orange tribal-print dress. Joyce had said I looked like an African samurai goddess.

As the night progressed and we drank more and more liquor, things got better. We were all having fun, but not as much as Taylor. She got tore up drinking moscato, Bacardi, and Grey Goose. The waitress had arranged a little surprise for her. She came out of the kitchen with a little birthday cake, and instead of everybody singing "Happy Birthday," they gave her a free lap dance as 50 Cent's "In Da Club" played and we all sang the lyrics.

"Go, go, go, go, go, go. Go, shawty. It's your birthday. We gon' party like it yo' birthday!"

All of us were shocked to see how much Taylor was getting into it while she recorded it all on her phone. The alcohol had her open all night. Just like I had thought, Joyce had lightened up and was now enjoying herself, but I could tell Denise was counting the seconds until we left. Me, I was good. I had always loved a good party, and it wasn't my first time in a strip club. But as usual, the turnup queen was doing the most. Taylor was slapping asses and pushing singles between G-strings. Pretty soon she was onstage dancing too.

We ended up staying until the club closed.

Somehow I dragged myself out of bed and went to class the next morning. I was taking a business management course at Clark Atlanta University. I had missed class last week, and no matter how hung over I was, I couldn't afford to miss another day. My economics instructor, Mr. Robert Baker, was putting me to sleep with his lecture. The struggle was definitely real as I tried to keep my eyes open, but I wasn't going to be disrespectful and put my head down on my desk.

Mr. Baker stood up behind his desk. "Okay, ladies and gentlemen, I want you to read chapters four and five this weekend, and we'll review them next Tuesday. Class is dismissed."

Everyone gathered their things and began to leave.

"Miss Haughton, may I speak to you for a moment?" Mr. Baker called as I gathered my things.

I stopped what I was doing and looked at him. "Sure."

He waited for the other students to leave before he spoke. He wore brown khakis with a brown blazer and a burgundy tie. His hair and mustache were neatly trimmed. He was a man who knew how to put himself together.

"I was wondering if you were going to make up the quiz you missed last week?" he said as I got to my feet.

"Oh, I'll be able to do that whenever you want me to."

He walked around his desk and over to where I was standing, As he stood in front of me, he said, "Well, normally, I don't let students make up quizzes, but you're one of my best. Lately, you seem a bit preoccupied, so I'm a little concerned."

"I'm sorry, Mr. Baker. It's been hard balancing all my classes. I think I may have taken on a little more than I can handle this semester."

He gave me a friendly smile. "It's okay. I understand. How about you come an hour before class on Tuesday and you can take the quiz then?"

I smiled. "That would be great. Thank you."

"No problem." He grinned. "You have a good night."

That was the first time we had really spoken to each other one-on-one, and that was the first time I had really paid attention to how attractive he was. He had pretty eyes, a gorgeous smile and, from what I could tell, a well-toned body. Until now, I hadn't even thought about him in a romantic way. I had just gotten out of a long-term relationship a few months ago and was enjoying my freedom. Mr. Baker was an attractive older man, but I was there to get my degree.

***

After class, I went over to Taylor's apartment to see how she was doing. I must have rung her doorbell twenty times before she answered. When the door finally swung open, she glared at me.

"Stop ringing the damn bell."

She looked like death warmed over. She was wearing a pair of boy shorts and a gray hoodie, and her red hair was a mess.

"I guess you're still fucked up?" I said as I stepped inside.

"My head is killing me. I'm never drinking like that again." Taylor shut the door, then stumbled back to her room and crawled back in bed. I followed behind her.

"It looks like you've been in here all day." A faint funk lingered in the air. "Smells like it too."

"Girl, the only place I've been is to the toilet to throw up."

I sat on her bed. "Oh, poor baby. You see why I didn't mix my drinks?"

"It's not fair. I was supposed to get laid last night," she groaned.

"Well, you almost did. The way you were bumping and grinding on them strippers, I'm pretty sure you would have got turned out."

Her eyebrows rose. "I was what?"

I smirked. "You don't remember what happened?"

"Really? I was dancing with strippers?"

"You really don't remember? You were swinging around the pole and everything!"

She smiled. "I was? Was I good?"

I couldn't help but laugh at her. "You were recording the whole night. You better not let that footage get out."

The doorbell rang repeatedly.

Taylor snapped, "Argh! Will you please tell them to stop ringing the doorbell? It's killing me!"

I got up and answered the door. It was Joyce and Denise. I had told them I was going to check on Taylor, and like clockwork, I knew they would be here to see the aftermath of last night's events. They came inside and followed me back to Taylor's room.

"Hey, guess what? Taylor doesn't remember what she did last night," I announced as I walked down the hallway.

Denise shook her head. "Figures."

"Hey, Taylor!" Joyce bellowed once we were inside her room.

"Stop yelling!" Taylor retorted angrily and pulled the covers up over her head.

Joyce flopped down next to her. "You don't remember what you did?" Then she burst into laughter.

Taylor rolled over and partially uncovered her face. "No, I don't."

Joyce continued to laugh. "Oh my God! Girl, you were shaking your ass like a hoefessional!"

Taylor uncovered the rest of her face, sat up, and smiled. "So that's why I woke up with all those dollar bills in my pants!"

We laughed.

"But you all had a good time, right? How 'bout you, Wallflower?" Taylor quizzed.

Denise glared at her. You could almost read the FUCK YOU sign flashing on her forehead. To be honest, Denise and Taylor were "friends" only because of me and Joyce. I didn't think they would ever be friends if it were not for us. I had hoped this would've changed by now, but I guessed that was only wishful thinking.

I picked up a pillow and threw it at Taylor. "Cut it out."

She shrugged. "I was just asking her a question."

"Yeah, it was great. Whoop-whoop," Denise said dryly.

"See, I told you." Taylor belched.

Joyce pushed her. "Ugh! My mouth was open, bitch!"

We spent the rest of the night laughing at Taylor's hung-over ass.

Chapter Two

Sweetest Taboo

RASHIDA

I spent the weekend at home, studying for the test I had on Tuesday. I was really not as focused as I should have been, so I had to cocoon myself from the outside world and social media.

Three days of studying paid off. I got to class early on Tuesday, and Mr. Baker was there waiting for me. He looked handsome in his brown blazer.

"I'm glad you made it," he said.

"I told you I would be here," I replied as I sat down at my desk.

He handed me a piece of paper, and I started to take the quiz. I could feel Robert staring at me as I worked. I had on a little black dress and had just shaved my legs that morning, so they looked extra smooth. For some reason, I felt turned on from having my teacher stare at me the way he was. He was becoming sexier to me by the second. Twenty-five minutes later I was done with the quiz. I got up, walked over to his desk, and handed him my paper.

"Here you go, Mr. Baker."

"Thank you." He looked it over before laying it on his desk.

"I think I'm the one who should be thanking you for letting me make this up."

"It was no problem," he replied. Mr. Baker stared into my eyes, and for a second, there was some real sexual chemistry between us.

Then people started to file into the classroom. Once everyone was seated and class began, I just sat there, fantasizing about Mr. Baker like a little schoolgirl, and I couldn't believe some of the thoughts that ran through my mind. My fantasies really started to turn me on. I felt myself becoming wet as I thought about how he would look naked. It was not like I hadn't had sex in a while. Maybe it was the fact that he was my instructor that turned me on. It was sorta taboo to be with him. I pushed those thoughts aside and focused on the class material. When the class was over, I gathered my books and rushed out of the room, intent on keeping Mr. Baker out of my mind.

But when I was walking to my car, I saw him again.

"Hello, Mr. Baker," I called out.

He turned and looked at me. "Hi. You can call me Robert," he said as he approached me.

"Oh, okay, Robert."

"Here you go, Miss. Haughton." He gave me back my quiz.

I saw an A in red at the top of the page. "Thank you."

"You don't have to thank me. You made the grade."

I smiled. "I guess I did . . . and, um, you can call me Rashida."

"Okay."

We stared at each for a moment and smiled.

"So where are you heading to, Miss Rashida?"

"Well, Robert"—I played with my hair—"I was heading home. And you?"

"I was going to go get a mocha latte. Would you mind joining me?"

"Sure. That sounds good."

There was a Starbucks on Spelman Lane, near Clark Atlanta. We walked inside, ordered our drinks, collected them, and found a seat in the back. The hum of cappuccino machines and light chatter filled the coffee shop as other customers sat around us, enjoying their drinks.

Robert stared at me and said, "You're very different from a lot of young women here in Atlanta."

"Really?" I smiled. "In what way?"

"Well, the way you carry yourself. You're very poised. Confident. Alluring, without being too overt."

I sipped my coffee. "Why, thank you, Robert. I've never heard a man describe me in such a dignified way."

"Even the way you speak, it's almost regal. Your speech pattern is distinctive and clear. A very rare thing here."

"Well, I think I owe that to my parents. My British father and Jamaican mother made sure my brother and I spoke proper English at all times." I smiled, reminiscing about them. "I can get ratchet when I want to, though."

He held up his hand. "Please don't."

I laughed. "I'll spare you."

"Thank you."

"Enough about me. Where are you from originally?"

"I was born and raised in Raleigh, North Carolina. Graduated summa cum laude from North Carolina State University, home of Wolfpack football. I taught at a high school before I eventually got a position teaching at my old university."

"Wow. Seems like you were doing good. What made you move to Atlanta?"

He exhaled and stared into his latte. "Well, after my divorce . . ." He glanced up at me. "I was ready for a complete change, and putting a state between me and my ex felt right. So two years later I'm a single bachelor living in a condo in the city."

I nodded. "How long were you married?"

"Thirteen years."

"Oh."

There was a moment of silence between us; then he continued. "Sometimes I feel the only good that came from it is our son, Quincy."

In that moment it became clear that I was dealing with a man with much more life experience than I had. Normally, finding all this out about a man I was into would be grounds for me to move on, but these experiences were normal for a man his age.

"I hope that doesn't make you wary of spending time with me," Robert confessed.

I shook my head. "No, not at all. Your past is your past. Everybody has one. I'm more interested in the future."

He smiled. "I concur."

For the next couple of weeks that became our routine after class. We would go to Starbucks, drink mocha lattes, and talk about life, music, or anything else that came to mind. Although it was nobody's business what we did outside of class, we were careful never to let anybody from the school see us together. We never did or said anything that wasn't platonic or professional, but there was always this underlying sexual attraction we had for one another. It wasn't until I had passed his class that things changed. We were in Starbucks one evening when it happened.

"This is to you, Rashida." He held up his coffee for a toast.

I held up mine. "Thank you, Robert."

"I guess this is the last night I get to share a hot coffee with you."

"Well, does it have to be?" I looked at him, and he knew what I meant.

He leaned forward in his chair. "I . . . I don't want this to be the last time I see you."

My eyes met his. "Me either."

"Well, you're no longer my student." He grinned, and I returned his smile.

"And you're no longer my professor."

He reached over and touched my hand. It seemed to me that all the bottled-up sexual tension was about to explode; then I felt myself becoming aroused.

"Well, I think I'm ready to go now," I announced.

He glanced at his watch. "Oh, okay."

"Are you coming with me?"

Robert smiled. "Yes, if you wish."

We got to my house at a little after nine. It was awkward as we sat in silence on the sofa. It was like we were tongue-tied and searching for the right words to say. I knew what I wanted, but I didn't want to rush it. The look on his face told me he wanted me too, but I could also see he was a bit taken aback by my house.

As he looked around the room from his spot on the sofa, he said, "This is a very nice place you have here."

"Thanks."

I didn't like telling people about my living situation. It always led to an awkward conversation on how I had acquired this place. I had bought this house two years ago, after I left the dorms over at Clark. I had wanted a place to call home, a place where I could raise a family someday. I decided to change the subject.

"Um, do you want something to drink?" I asked him.

"Uh, no, I'm fine." Once again, his eyes scanned his surroundings. "May I ask you a question? And I hope you won't get offended."

I smiled. "I won't."

"Do you live with your parents?"

I shook my head. "No, this is my house."

"How can a college student afford a place like this?"

That was a question I was asked a lot by people who visited. My house sat on a one-acre lot and had a pool and a private backyard. The main level had an open kitchen, a spacious living room, and a den with a vaulted beamed ceiling and sliding glass doors that opened to a large deck. The house had a fully finished basement with a theater, a bedroom, and a bath. And upstairs there were six bedrooms and four bathrooms. I guessed it was a bit more extravagant than the average home.

"My brother and I inherited some money when my parents died. I was fourteen at the time."

Robert exhaled. "I'm sorry. I shouldn't have asked you."

"It's okay. You didn't know. I know it's a bit unusual for someone my age to have a place like this, but I like having the space."

He looked at me anxiously. "Well, here we are."

"Why is this so awkward now?"

"I don't know. Maybe it's because we're not in the classroom or at Starbucks."

I smiled nervously. "I guess we're both out of our comfort zone."

He reached over and took my hand. "I guess so. Perhaps we should make a new one?" He leaned over slowly and kissed me.

All the butterflies in my stomach started to fly. It was amazing how fast I got aroused from just one kiss. I slid my hand up Robert's leg and felt his stiffening penis.

Soon his hand was up my dress, pulling my panties to the side, touching me. His fingers caressed me, and it felt so good. The more wet kisses we exchanged, the more we fondled each other. My breathing became heavier, and my sexual noises encouraged him to go further. Pretty soon two fingers were sliding inside me.

Before it went any further, I took his hand. "Come with me."

I stood up, and Robert followed me to my bedroom, where he began to undress me. His hands caressed my breasts, and he kissed my nipples. He unbuttoned his pants and found his erection. It wasn't too long, but it was thick. He undressed himself as I lay back on the bed. He took a condom from his wallet, rolled it on, then climbed on top of me. First, he kissed my forehead, kissed my lips, licked my neck, and then pushed inside me. I watched his erection sink inside me and fill me up. Robert took his time, stroked me nice and slow. He was a man of experience, a man who wasn't just trying to get his. He understood the difference between making love and fucking.

Being penetrated made me feel good. Pretty soon his slow stroke tempo turned into rapid thrusts, and I started to buck up and down. I felt his erection hit a spot that made me groan. I could feel my wetness seeping between the cheeks of my ass. We rolled over, and with me on top, I rode his stiffness. My wetness was all over his manhood.

Robert closed his eyes and moaned. He gripped my waist, trying to hold on, trying to prevent his load from exploding, but when I leaned back and danced on his penis, he lost control. He roared like a wounded animal, shivered, then pulled me down on top of him and held me close. Our lips touched, and we held each other, allowing our orgasms to flow simultaneously. I gave him my sexual youth, and he gave me his experience. It was a fair exchange of energy, a release that we both needed.

He caressed my face. "I don't normally do this."

"Do what?"

"Sleep with my former students."

I smiled. "Then I feel special. So what happens now?"

"I would like to see you again, if you don't mind."

"That would be nice."

He frowned. "Are you sure you don't mind being with a man my age?"

"You're not that old, Robert."

"But the gap in years is enough to raise eyebrows."

"I know, and if that bothered me, we wouldn't be here now."

He grinned. "You're like no other woman I've ever met, Rashida."

"And you're certainly one of a kind. The kind of man I want to spend my days and nights with."

We kissed each other again.

After that night we officially began dating. Although ours was not a committed relationship, we agreed to take things slowly and see where it all led.

Although he had his own place, Robert spent the next few weeks at my house, and it felt like he had moved in. I enjoyed his company, but I wasn't in love with him. Maybe that head-over-heels feeling would come in time, so I decided that until then, I would keep all my options open.

Chapter Three

Only For the Night

RASHIDA

Robert and I had been dating for about a month, but I still enjoyed hanging out with my girls. The Gold Room was the spot where we liked to unwind on a Friday night, but as it turned out, tonight I was going solo. Robert was out of town visiting his son for the weekend in North Carolina. I had called my girls, but they were all busy. Joyce had an exam on Monday morning and needed to study. Denise opted to just stay home, and Taylor had a date. So tonight it was just me, and I wanted to dance, drink, and have some fun.

As soon as I entered the Gold Room, I walked up to the bar, took a seat, and ordered a drink. The bartender obliged, and soon I was sipping on a Hpnotiq martini and in a zone. The music was right, and the lights were down low, except for the occasional purple and blue bulbs throughout. The huge chandelier in the center of the club's ceiling was alternating colors, while a fog machine pumped out white clouds, which spread across the floor. The place was half-packed, with groups of ladies on the dance floor, and a few men were looking at them over the railing on the second level. I finished my drink, and the bartender brought me another one.

I stared at him oddly as he placed the glass in front of me. "Who's this from?"

"From the gentleman over there." He pointed toward a man sitting at a booth in the corner.

I could tell right away this was game. When the bartender walked away, the man got up and effortlessly walked over to me. I knew this wasn't the first time he'd done this, but I was impressed nevertheless with his high degree of confidence. As he got closer, I could see he had a medium build and a well-toned body. He was about six-one, maybe six-two, with a mocha complexion and a curly 'fro. Dark jeans, a white button down, matching all-white Nikes, and a gray blazer made him look like his was modeling for *Esquire*.

When he spoke, he sounded quite articulate. "I know this is a bit of a cliché, but when I saw you sitting there, I couldn't resist. I hope you don't mind."

His sexy five o'clock shadow completed the package, and I smiled. "I don't. It's nice to know I still have that kind of effect on men."

"Still? C'mon, I know I'm not the first man to buy you a drink."

"No, but it's still nice when it happens."

"Well, I'm glad I was able to put a smile on your face."

I grinned. "Well, I know I'm not the first woman you ever bought a drink for."

He gave me a sexy grin. "No, but you are the finest I ever did it for."

He was confident without being arrogant. I liked that. I could feel his eyes all over my body. Being able to captivate a man's attention was a turn-on. His stare seemed to penetrate straight into me. Not too many men were able to make me blush, but he did.

"My name is Alonzo."

I couldn't help but think how fine this man was, and his smile was so sexy. By the way he moved, I decided he was a street dude, but he sure knew how to carry himself like a gentleman.

I smiled. "I'm Rashida."

"Nice to meet you, Rashida."

"Nice meeting you too. So what else do you do, other than buy women drinks?" I took a sip of my Hpnotiq.

"You don't know who I am?"

I was a bit dumbfounded by his question. Was his ego about to ruin the good start he was off to? "I'm sorry, should I?"

Alonzo smiled. "I'm Alonzo Hall from WHXZ. *The Quiet Storm* show at midnight?"

"Oh, I'm sorry, but I don't really listen to the radio much at night."

He grinned. "Too busy getting that beauty sleep."

I smiled at his corny line. He was lucky he was sexy. "Something like that."

"So tell me, Rashida, what do you do?"

"I'm a student at Clark for now. Business major."

He nodded. "I like that."

"Really? So if I said I worked at Strokers, would you still be impressed?"

He looked me up and down. "Yes, as long as your long-term goals entailed something beyond swinging on a pole, I would be. But there's something about you that seems way too classy to be there."

"But if I was?"

He smiled. "I think I would become your biggest tipper."

We laughed and stared into each other's eyes. There was energy and chemistry between us. The way he looked and his quick wit stimulated me. "Pretty Wings" by Maxwell began to play, and Alonzo glanced at the dance floor.

"So, would you like to dance?" he asked me.

I nodded and took another sip of my drink. "Sure."

We walked out to the dance floor and started to dance. I turned around and slowly ground my behind on him. I felt him becoming hard. Inhaling his intoxicating cologne, I felt myself relax as he rubbed his big, soft hands over my shoulders and down to my waist. It felt good being in his embrace. I turned around and faced him, bringing my lips inches away from his. I wanted this scenario to play out, but it didn't. After the song ended, he held my hand gently, and we walked back to the bar.

"You're a good dancer," I told him.

"I'm only as good as my partner."

"Do you have a regular partner?" I asked coolly.

"Not in a while."

I nodded. We both knew what was coming next. I was anticipating yet dreading it at the same time. Why did I have to meet him now? Where was he two months ago?

"So since I like to dance and you're not dancing at Strokers"—we both chuckled—"how about I call you sometime?" he asked.

I looked at Alonzo with disappointment in my eyes. My mind drifted to Robert, and I had to admit I felt a little guilty. "I don't want you to think I'm blowing you off, but I've just started seeing somebody."

Alonzo stared at me for a moment, still holding my hand, as if he would give anything to change what he had just heard me say. Just then, I reminded myself that Robert and I weren't in a committed relationship, so why should I let Alonzo just walk away?

I almost wished there was a way to change what I had said or at least take my words back.

He sighed. "Oh, lucky guy. Well, uh, it was nice dancing with you." Alonzo slowly let go of my hand, and I closed my eyes, saddened by this turn of events.

"Thank you for the drink. I'll try to catch your show," I told him.

He nodded. "The mo' listeners, the mo' ratings, the mo' betta." He started to walk away, and I did something that surprised me.

"I wouldn't mind another dance," I called.

Alonzo turned, smiled at me, took my hand, and led me back to the dance floor, where we held each other close. It didn't matter what song was playing; we held on to each other like it was the same slow jam on repeat. Feeling his body next to mine was making me have so many wild notions, and the fleeting thought "What if I had met him first?" crossed my mind. Once again, our lips were inches away. Only this time I gave in to my lust and kissed him. It was wrong for me to cross this line, but I didn't care. I had always been faithful in my relationships, but this time I felt something different and didn't want to let it go. I couldn't. I was tired of always being responsible, always doing the right thing. Tonight I just wanted it to be all about me. I gazed into his eyes, and we both knew what we wanted.

"I'm ready to go if you are," I told him.

He smiled. "Yeah."

I followed him out of the club, we both got in our separate cars, and then I trailed him in mine to a nice two-story house on the south side of Atlanta. The entire drive from the club, I had time to reconsider what I was going to do.

Robert's a good guy, I thought to myself.

What does that have to do with anything? my rational mind retorted. *You're not married.*

I'm trying to make this work, I insisted.

Why? You don't have a commitment to him. It's only been a month.

My mind drifted back to Alonzo and how he had made me feel on the dance floor. *Fuck it.* It was him I wanted. There was no reason for me not to be with him tonight.

I pulled into his driveway and got out just as he was closing his car door. He took my hand, led me to the front door, and we went inside. I noticed a couple of jazz-inspired art pieces on the walls: Duke Ellington in a colorful piece and Miles Davis in another. The black-and-white painting of Aaliyah was beautiful. He had a spacious living room, with oversized plush furniture and a state-of-the-art entertainment system. I liked his style, but I wasn't here for the décor.

"Do you want something to drink?" he asked me.

I smiled. "No."

He smiled too, and his eyes met mine.

I walked over to his staircase and looked up. "You live here alone?"

"My best friend, Sean, lives here too. He's out of town right now."

I raised an eyebrow at him. "You sure about that?"

He chuckled and walked toward me. "Yep, no girl-friend, no kids, just us. I like having room to live."

Normally, I wouldn't believe a guy if he said that, but I did believe him. I felt the same way about having plenty of living space. He pulled me close and kissed me with so much passion, then took me upstairs to his bedroom. What happened next was simply the most intense love-making I had ever experienced. A night I would never forget.

Two months later . . .

My night with Alonzo was special, but afterward I decided not to call him again. If I did, I didn't think

I would ever leave him. As much as I tried to deny it, I still felt guilty because of Robert. He didn't deserve what I had done. After that night I decided it was best to focus on us and really try to make things work.

Tonight we were hosting dinner at my house, and after I got dressed, I began fixing my hair in the mirror.

"You look beautiful." Robert walked up behind me and rubbed my shoulders.

"Thanks. You're not too shabby yourself, Professor."

"So who am I meeting tonight?"

"I told you, my best friend in the whole world. Joyce."

"Okay, so is your friend gonna hate me or what?"

I stopped styling my hair and looked at him in the mirror.

"What? Joyce is gonna like you. So is Denise. Now my other close friend, Taylor, she's the temperamental one."

He sighed. "That's great to hear."

As if on cue, the doorbell rang, and I headed to the front door, with Robert behind me. I glanced back at him. "Don't worry. Everything's gonna be fine."

I opened the door, and my jaw hit the floor. There he was, in front of me again, just as handsome as ever. Alonzo was standing on my doorstep, with Joyce by his side. What the hell was he doing here with her? The smile on his face evaporated. He was just as stunned to see me. I couldn't speak for a second; then I forced out a high-pitched greeting.

"Oh my . . . Hi!"

Joyce smiled. "Hey. Alonzo, this is my best friend in the whole world, Rashida."

Alonzo swallowed hard. "Hello."

"Rashida, this is Alonzo."

We both knew we had no choice but to play along.

He extended his hand, and I shook it. "Nice to meet you."

He played along, saying, "It's nice to meet you too."

This was crazy. How did he end up with Joyce? More importantly, should I tell her what happened between us?

Chapter Four

Seems Like You're Ready

ALONZO

She was the last person I was expecting Joyce to introduce me to. She had always referred to her friend as 'Shida. I had no idea that this was the Rashida I had met two months ago at the Gold Room. I could never forget the love we had made that night or how much I had wanted her to stay.

Here I was standing in her living room, staring at her beautiful face, as she stood next to her boyfriend, Robert. I could tell by the look in her eyes she didn't want Joyce to know the truth, so I played along with it.

This was so damn awkward. After that night I really didn't think I would see her again, and after I met Joyce, Rashida was just a pleasant afterthought. It figured that beautiful women like Joyce and Rashida ran together. Best friends, no less. Just my luck. Over the next few hours, the four of us made small talk, but I avoided eye contact with Rashida.

Joyce and I left finally, and as we drove down the street, Joyce could sense by my quietness that something was off, and decide to talk to me.

"So, what did you think of my friend?"

"Rashida? Oh, she's nice."

Joyce stared at me for a moment. "That's it? Just nice?"

I shrugged. "Yeah, I mean, what are you expecting me to say?"

She sighed. "Nothing, I guess. I was just expecting you to say more than that."

"Sorry. I just got a lot on my mind." I wasn't lying about that. "But Rashida seems like a very nice girl. Her dude seems a bit uptight, though."

Joyce nodded. "Yeah, he does. He's not the type of guy she normally dates."

"Oh really? What's her type?"

"Um, we normally have similar taste in men. So maybe a guy kinda like you," she answered.

I exhaled. "Oh, okay."

"Robert seems okay, but I don't see Rashida being with him for too long. Maybe you could hook her up with one of your boys. How about Sean?"

I shook my head. "Uh, I don't think Sean is the right kinda of guy for her. Don't get me wrong. He's a good dude, but he's a playa. He's like a hawk out hunting women."

Joyce smirked at me. "Hmm. They say birds of a feather flock together, so are you playing games with me?"

I grinned. "Nah, I'm not about that life anymore. There just comes a time when you want something real. Besides, I would never play with your heart."

"That's good to know." She smiled. "But I hope there are other parts of my body you'd like to play with."

She slid her hand up my thigh and rested it on my crotch, where she found something nice and hard. Now, don't get me wrong; despite this awkward situation with Rashida, Joyce was a sexy woman that any man would do anything to get with. I knew because I damn near did too.

We had met each other six weeks ago, while we were in line at Target. I was picking up a few Blu-rays and was standing behind her, admiring the view of her voluptuous behind. She spotted me checking her out. I could tell by the grin on her face that she didn't mind me looking. Her tight red skirt left nothing to the imagination, so I started a little small talk, which we continued as we headed out to the parking lot. We exchanged numbers, and a few days later we went out.

Since then, we'd had nights at the movies, dinner dates at different restaurants, and now dinner at her best friend's. It had been all good, but we hadn't had sex yet. Not that I was in a rush, but she liked to tease me, and that was something I didn't like. We would go so far before she would stop. If I were the same guy I was a few years ago, I would have ended things after the second time she pulled that on me, but I was trying to be a better man these days.

I drove her back to her apartment in Druid Hills and walked her to the door. She took out her keys, opened her front door, then looked at me.

"Would you like to come in?" she asked.

I just stood there, considering her invitation. She could see the hesitation on my face. I wasn't in the mood to be played with tonight.

"Uh, I'm not sure I should," I said at last.

She took my hand and pulled me toward her. "C'mon."

I went inside and had a seat on the sofa. *Here we go again*, I thought. I knew the routine already. I would go inside and get comfortable. She would get us some drinks, such as the Italian Nivuro she loved. Then she would join me on the sofa, we'd make small talk, and then we'd get to kissing and touching. And then she would say, "We can't do this yet." Then I would be left hanging with Nivuro on my lips and a painful erection in my jeans.

If tonight was going to be more of the same, I wasn't going for it. Joyce turned on some Miguel from a playlist on her cell, and it flowed through the wireless speakers on the mantel. She stood in front of me as I sat on the sofa.

"Would you like a drink?" she asked.

I sighed. "Nah, I'm good."

She looked at me and slightly raised her eyebrow without saying a word. I said nothing, and in this uncomfortable silence, I was sure Joyce could sense my frustration.

That was the first time I had turned down her offer for a nightcap. I wasn't trying to repeat the same thing we had done over and over. Truth be told, our dinner with Rashida was still on my mind. Of all the women in the world Joyce could be best friends with, it had to be her.

"I'ma go freshen up a bit. I'll be just a minute." She headed toward her bedroom.

"Yeah. Sure, okay."

The bedroom door closed, and I sat there for a moment thinking about everything. The situation with Rashida was unsettling, and I couldn't deny the attraction I still had to her. Joyce was a good girl, but everything was hitting too close to home. Maybe a relationship wasn't the right thing for us.

"Joyce?" I called out. I had made up my mind it was best to leave. There was no sense in dragging this out any further.

When I got no response, I stood up and headed toward the bedroom door to end things. Just as I reached the door, it opened. There was Joyce, standing before me in a black-lace bra and panty set. My mouth fell open. She looked like she had just stepped off the pages of a *Playboy* editorial spread.

She stepped closer to me. "I know I've given you some mixed signals, and I know you've been frustrated. I just had to be sure this wasn't all a game for you."

"It's not."

"I know that now."

She kissed me. It was the type of kiss that was an invitation to enjoy everything before me. It was an invitation I gladly accepted. My hands rubbed her soft skin. Fingers caressed her back and found her supple ass cheeks to squeeze. She kissed my chin. Her tongue eased out of her mouth and tasted my neck. Her breathing was rapid, almost out of control. A pair of soft breasts pressed against my chest, and in my jeans her hand found my sudden erection, which was dying to be set free. She unbuckled my belt, then unfastened my jeans.

"Slow down," I whispered. "We don't have to rush."

My words fell on deaf ears, because she didn't stop until her hand found the hardness in my boxers. Her hand fondled and stroked my penis, making me growl. She had awakened a beast inside me, a part of me that was dying to be set free. An animal that would show no mercy with the things it would do to her. My jeans fell to mid-thigh, allowing her to pull my boxers down over my ass. My ridged hardness pressed against the lacy material of her panties, damn near pushing inside her.

I whispered, "Are you sure?"

"Yes."

My hands cupped her ass, and I hoisted her up on me. She wrapped her legs around my waist. After kicking off my shoes, I carried her inside her bedroom and laid her on the edge of the queen-size bed. Her long legs dangled over the edge. They say the way a person kept their bedroom was a reflection who they were. It was their most intimate and personal space. I quickly took in my surroundings. This was my first time entering her sanctuary; it was flawless, just like her.

I stared at her long, lean body; her black panties could barely contain her thickness inside. Her golden-brown skin was unblemished and smooth. I finished undressing myself and took a condom out of my wallet. Her full, succulent breasts rising and falling with each anxious breath, Joyce kept her eyes on me as I rolled on the Magnum.

She unclasped her bra and tossed it to the side. I gazed at a pair of beautiful brown breasts with dark areolas and hard nipples. I licked my lips. She smiled. I pulled her moist panties down over her long legs; then she parted her thighs, showing me where she wanted me to be. I climbed on top of her, then kissed her inner thighs as I traveled down into her valley. I drank from the pool between her legs, which quickly became a river. Soft moans left her lips, and her back arched in excitement. I ate her alive like I was a zombie on *The Walking Dead*. Her sweetness drenched my face, and her hands pulled at the sheets. My grip on her legs did not allow her to escape the sweet torture I was giving her.

"Oh, my gawd . . . Alonzo . . . I'm cumming . . . I'm . . . I'm . . . aah . . ."

Another moan escaped her throat, and that victory cry let me know she had arrived at the promised land. Her legs curled back, and uncontrollable spasms made her body shudder. She panted and whined in pleasure. Her breathing was out of control. She was almost done, but I had only just begun. I left her valley on fire, traveled to her mountains, and sucked on erect nipples. My penis rubbed her clit.

"What . . . are you . . . trying to do . . . to me?" she gasped.

"What do you *want* me to do?"

"Anything . . . everything."

"Tell me how much you want it."

"Damn you."

It was my time to tease. "I could stop."

"No! Please! Give it to me!"

"You want it?"

"Yes, please!"

"Okay."

I slowly entered her and watched as her beautiful face made an ugly expression. Joyce was on fire. I felt her wetness surround me. I stroked her deeply and made sure I touched the bottom of her love. More moans and groans from both of us filled the air. Our bodies shifted around the bed as we tried to find the perfect angle. Joyce gave me her all. The classy girl I had met a month ago was now this sex goddess doing things to me I thought about only in my wildest dreams.

After that night it was on and popping on the regular. She wanted it every chance she got, and I was more than happy to give it to her. Our relationship became stronger, but I knew it would be just a matter of time before I saw Rashida again.

And I was right. Rashida invited us to her house for a Memorial Day cookout. The first time we went over there for dinner, I had assumed that the house was Robert's, but then Joyce had clarified that it was, in fact, Rashida's home. She explained that Rashida and her brother had received a large settlement after her parents' death.

We arrived at the cookout fashionably late, and once again it was weird to see Rashida. Robert was at the grill, with a nice crowd of folks talking and drinking around him. Joyce and I mingled after greeting our hosts. After we had strolled around a bit, I wanted a beer and went over to the cooler to retrieve one, but it was empty. Robert told me there was a case of beer in the refrigerator, so I went inside the house to fetch it.

When I entered the kitchen, Rashida was over by the stove, checking on some of the food on the burners. She looked good in the floor-length African-print skirt and the fuchsia-colored bandeau she wore. As I contemplated the style of her skirt, I recognized it as a Nigerian Ankara print. I was feeling her style. She turned just then and saw me standing there. We stared at each other for a second, both of us thinking the same thing. I decided to break the ice.

"So are we going to pretend like it never happened?"

She smiled. "I guess not. Kind of a big elephant in the room, huh?"

"Very big," I agreed. "Looks like we're going to be around each other a lot, and I wanted to clear the air. I just don't want anything to be awkward."

"So things between you and Joyce are good?"

I nodded. "Yes, they are."

"I'm happy for you two." She turned to stir a pot on the stove.

"Rashida, I wasn't expecting ever to see you again."

"I understand," she admitted, her back facing me. "That night was just for us, something we both needed at the time. There's nothing to explain." She turned back toward me and extended her hand. "Friends?"

I shook her hand. "Friends."

Chapter Five

A Girl Like Me

DENISE

I knew I was not the girl every man was tripping over themselves to get with, nor did I want to be that chick. I saw the way men look at Rashida, Joyce, and especially Taylor, and I could do without that kind of attention. Not that I was some kind of ugly duckling, but I just didn't try to put myself out there like that.

I'd been friends with Rashida and Joyce since high school. Taylor was more of a friend by default than by choice. I didn't hate her; I just didn't really have anything in common with her. Our personalities were polar opposites. I'd tried to become closer to her, but she was just too damn ghetto for my liking. She dressed like a video ho and then wanted to call me Wallflower because I chose to dress like a lady. Whatever!

I already knew when Rashida said she was going to have a cookout at her house for Memorial Day that Taylor was going to be underdressed for the occasion. And there she was, forty-five minutes late, as usual, walking up to us, wearing a red miniskirt that barely covered her ass and a matching bikini top, with her breasts bouncing with every step. She had recently dyed her hair blond, which complemented her complexion.

"Seriously? She couldn't put on some clothes?" I muttered.

Rashida chuckled. "You're acting as if this is your first time meeting Taylor. Relax and don't start any drama."

I rolled my eyes. "I never do."

Rashida shook her head. I knew she always tried to stay neutral in our disagreements, but she couldn't just ignore all the ratchet shit Taylor pulled. There was a nice crowd of people here already, and a lot of them were our friends from Clark Atlanta, others were people who worked in the entertainment industry in Atlanta, and some were Rashida's family members. Most of the men were rubbernecking in Taylor's direction, trying to get a glance at her ass as she walked through. Robert was at the grill, while Rashida and I were sat on foldout chairs, with a few others standing by us. A handful of the people here were Robert's coworkers. A few of them were here with their wives, who didn't like the way their husbands were gawking at Taylor.

Rashida got up to greet her. "Hey, sexy gal," she called. "You're gonna get somebody's man in trouble, walking around here with all that ass under that skirt."

"I can't help it if they like what they see," Taylor said nonchalantly and glanced back at a couple of men still ogling her. "Besides, I'm here for the food! Where the ribs at?"

"Robert just took a rack of ribs off the grill." Rashida pointed to a table nearby that had the food on it. "Go help yourself."

"Say less," Taylor said and made her way toward the food.

Joyce was with her new boyfriend, Alonzo, and they were all booed up. He was an attractive man. They looked cute together. He had come to the cookout with a male friend, who was also cute, but I could tell by the way he was dressed—like a wannabe rapper—that he was definitely not my type. As Taylor went over to the table with the food, I could still see a bunch of men staring at her ass and whispering to each other. Disgusting. Even the men here with their significant others were still trying to sneak a peek.

My eyes went back over to where Joyce and Alonzo were standing, and I saw that his boy wasn't staring at Taylor at all. He was staring directly at me. We made eye contact and held it for a good ten seconds. A smile came across his face. I got self-conscious and quickly looked away. He was wearing a black wife beater and skinny jeans. A silver chain was around his neck, with a large crucifix hanging from it. His hair was neatly cornrowed to the back. He looked rough but sexy at the same time. But why was he checking me out like that? He was not the type of guy that paid me any attention. I got up and headed toward Rashida, who was talking to Taylor.

"Wus up, Denise?" Taylor looked me up and down. "On your way to Bible study after this?"

I glared at her. I had on a floral-print dress that stopped just past my knees. I wasn't showing my ass to everyone. I looked appropriate for the occasion. "Hey, Taylor. Nice outfit. Strolling down Bankhead afterward?"

Rashida sighed. "Must you two go at each other's throats as soon as you see each other?"

I looked at Rashida. "I told you she starts it."

Taylor rolled her eyes. "Please! Don't act like you weren't whispering shit about me to Rashida as soon as you saw me. I know I look good. Don't hate."

"I'm not hating on you, but aren't you the slightest bit concerned with how these men are gawking at you?"

Taylor smirked. "Men are gonna look regardless. Besides, I'm comfortable in my own skin." She looked over at Sean. "Speaking of which, you certainly have some fine ones here, 'Shida. Who's that next to Joyce and Alonzo?"

Rashida glanced in that direction. "Oh, that's Alonzo's homeboy, Sean."

Taylor smiled. "Well, isn't he cute? I should welcome him to the party."

I shook my head. Despite all the decent-looking single brothers here, of course, Taylor had zeroed in on the one who looked like he was in G-Unit. I just didn't get her.

For the rest of the cookout, I chilled near the house, sipping on a Heineken, watching some fellas playing spades. Rashida was doing her best to make sure everyone was enjoying themselves. Joyce was sitting on Alonzo's lap, and of course, Taylor had made her way over to Sean and was now flirting with him. He seemed like he was into her. What man wouldn't be feeling a girl who looked like Taylor, especially if she was all touchy-feely with him? I shook my head and went back to enjoying the cookout.

By the time the sun started going down, most of the people had left. Joyce had left with Alonzo, and Taylor was nowhere in sight. I opted to stick around and help Rashida clean up. There were a few people sitting around the grill, and Robert was eating and drinking as he chatted with them. Rashida told me they were some of Robert's coworkers. They were all a bit older than us: I figured they were in their forties or fifties. It didn't seem like Rashida was too interested in what they were talking about. I had never thought Rashida would date an older man, but I guessed you liked what you liked.

I took a bag of trash outside from the kitchen, and as I was walking toward the trash bins, I saw him. He was the last person I expected to still be here.

"Hey. How you doing?" he asked.

"I'm fine."

He noticed the bag in my hand. "Let me help you with that."

I nodded, and he politely took the trash from me and dumped it in a bin.

"Thank you."

"You're welcome. You're Denise, right?"

"Yeah." I was surprised. "How do you know my name?"

"Joyce was telling me about her friends."

"Oh, okay." I stared at his handsome face. He was so sexy up close and personal. "Well, it is nice meeting you."

"My name is Sean."

"I know."

"I saw you earlier by yourself. I was wondering if you came here solo."

"Why?" I quizzed.

"Well, you looked kind of lonely."

What the hell? I thought. *I know this wannabe thug isn't over here taking pity on me like I'm some lost kitten in need of some attention.*

"Listen, Sean, I don't really know you like that, and you definitely don't know me, so it's a bit inappropriate to be having this discussion with you. Excuse me." I turned to leave, and he quickly jogged in front of me.

"Whoa! Hold up, Ma. I didn't mean to offend you. I just wanna get to know you."

I stared at him oddly. "Me? You wanna get to know *me*? Why?"

He grinned. "Because I'm feeling you and would like to take you out sometime."

I was a bit speechless. It was not that I wasn't used to guys asking me out. I did date, but guys like Sean never asked me out. This had to be some kind of joke.

"You want to take me out? Why me? Weren't you flirting with Taylor not too long ago?"

He nodded. "She's cool people, but she's not really my type."

I laughed. "She's not? But I am? Yeah, okay."

"Why is that so hard for you to believe? Listen, Ma, I ain't trying to waste your time, so if you ain't feeling me, I'll leave you alone."

"Wait. You're serious, aren't you?"

"Yes, I am. I just wanna get to know you. Maybe I could call you sometime, and we can get to know each other better. No pressure."

"Okay," I said, blushing. "We can do that."

"Cool."

He pulled out his phone. I gave him my number, and he punched it in. Sean was not at all what I expected from a man who looked like him. And the more I gazed at his fine chocolate self, the more I found myself becoming aroused. Why was he so damn sexy? Pretty brown eyes, perfect white teeth, muscular arms and chest. The smelled of his Versace cologne made me want to get closer.

He gave me a hug as he said goodbye, and Lord knows I wanted to melt in his arms. Part of me still didn't believe this was happening to me. Another part of me couldn't wait for Taylor to see me with Sean. I'd show her that I didn't have be damn near naked to get a man.